D1571515

*Modern Jewish
Literature and Culture*

Robert A. Mandel, series editor

for JoAnne

The American Sun & Wind Moving Picture Company

For Estella
a literary Lubbock
with admiration
& Joy

Jay

5/13

Jay Neugeboren

Texas Tech University Press

The first chapter of this novel, in somewhat different form, appeared in *News From The New American Diaspora* (2005).

This book is typeset in Palatino Linotype. The paper used in this book meets the minimum requirements of ANSI/NISO Z39.48-1992 (R1997).
∞

Designed by Kasey McBeath

This book is catalogued with the Library of Congress.
ISBN (cloth): 978-0-89672-779-3
ISBN (e-book): 978-0-89672-780-9

Printed in the United States of America
13 14 15 16 17 18 19 20 21 / 9 8 7 6 5 4 3 2 1

Texas Tech University Press
Box 41037 I Lubbock, Texas 79409-1037 USA
800.832.4042 I ttup@ttu.edu I www.ttupress.org

1915

In the forest, high above the lake, I imagined that I was, far below, trapped beneath the black ice. I gathered sticks for kindling, pressed them close to my chest, then brought the bundle, like a gift, to the edge of the woods. I looked down at the lake and saw that Mister Lesko and his horse were already on the ice, clouds of steam pouring from the horse's nostrils.

Beside the small fire, my Uncle Ben was unwrapping the camera from its blanket—lifting it tenderly, as if it were an infant—then setting it upon the tripod: a sign that we would soon begin. I closed my eyes and prayed that I wasn't too late—that I had not stayed in the forest too long, and that there was still time for me to help make up our new story.

I could make a story out of anything back then—a nail, a glass, a shoe, a tree, a mirror, a button, a window, a wall—and for every story I made up and gave away, I also made one up that I told no one about—one I stored inside me, in the rooms where I kept my most precious memories and pictures.

Below me, Mister Lesko was hitching his horse to the ice plow, and when he urged his horse forward I climbed into his head and saw that he was hoping the horse would resist him so that he might use his whip. The sleighs—pungs, we called them—were on the land, next to the ice house, and while I was gone, Mister Lesko and his son had cut a runway into the lake's shallow end for floating the cakes of ice to shore.

I closed my eyes, made a picture of the lake, and I labeled the picture as if I were back at our studio, printing out an opening title for one of the moving pictures my family made:

FORT LEE, NEW JERSEY
NOVEMBER 17, 1915

I opened my eyes and the lake was still there. My Uncle Ben was fishing inside his suitcase for his lenses and film. My mother was lifting dresses and hats from the clothing bag my father held open for her. My Uncle Karl was talking with Mister Lesko, showing him where he wanted the ice cut.

I made my way down the hill, and started across the lake to where the fire was burning below the camera. I had helped build it there—lit the first match to the greasy newspapers— so that, the heat rising steadily, the oil in the camera would remain soft and the gears would not freeze.

I looked down into the black ice—the first ice of winter—veined like marble, clear like glass. In the space between land and snow, I knew, small animals and insects lived all winter long. I wondered if there was a space like that between water and ice where I might lie down.

Ben held a blue lens to his eye, so he could remove colors from the world and know what our story would look like in black and white. In ancient times, Ben had taught me, men would build memory palaces inside their minds, and in each of the palace's rooms they would keep furniture, and on the furniture they would place objects. They invented systems and conjured up images by which they could name the rooms, and recall which rooms contained which objects and how the rooms led to and from one another. Sometimes they did this to remember the objects themselves, and sometimes the objects were there to remind them of other objects, or of lists or texts they wanted to set to heart: of the words to the Psalms, or the names of the saints, or where all the stars in the universe were located.

In our own times, Ben said, people still organized their memories in similar ways, but now instead of being kings, priests, or philosophers, they were magicians, memory artists, or *idiot savants* working in vaudeville, or at county fairs, or in circuses.

My father's three suitcases, like steps leading to an invisible stage, sat side by side on the ice, next to the sleds on which we transported our equipment, and inside the suitcases were his accordion, his violin, and his clarinet. When Karl wanted actors and actresses to show particular feelings, he had my father play music for them. My father played the violin during love scenes. He played the accordion during bar room scenes and cowboy movies. He played the clarinet or a small pump-organ for night scenes, or when people were dying.

I deposited my bundle of sticks next to the fire. Ben tapped the side of the camera. Is this one reel? he asked.

No, I said. It's not real until you open the shutter, turn the handle, and let the light inside.

Stop with the nonsense, Karl said. Two reels. This one's a two-reeler we have to finish by the end of the week.

Ben winked at me. But if it's too real, I asked, how will we be able to bear it?

And we don't need your crappy routines either, you two, Karl snapped. If I want your opinion, I'll give it to you.

Leave the boy alone, my father said. He's a good boy, even if he looks like a girl.

Mister Lesko's son was on the ice now, but I couldn't tell which was the father and which the son. They both wore beaver coats, the fur turned to the inside, and black leather hats with earlaps. One of them walked on the far side of the horse, pushing an ice-marker back and forth along the surface of the lake, making a checkerboard of squares.

Ben's warm breath was on my face. Joey? he asked.

I closed my eyes and the world filled with light. I waited,

and watched the ice and sky turn to a pale ivory color, like melted bones.

I see a woman drowning, I said.

And? Karl asked. So she's drowning. So what else?

I see her drowning, I said, and she's caught inside a hole in the ice, trying to climb out, to save herself.

And then—? Karl asked.

There's a man, and he has a whip in his hand.

I looked at the hill where I had been a short while before, and I pointed. There's a child up there, alone, in the forest.

Why? Ben asked.

Because the woman had to marry the man after she gave birth to their child. But the man beat the child, and one day, when it was old enough, it ran away.

I like it, Karl said. This we can sell—whips, and a mother and child we can weep for, and then a chase.

Whipping and weeping, my father said brightly. Weeping and whipping. He shrugged. Whoopee, he added, softly.

My mother put her arm around his neck. What else, sweetheart? she asked me.

Well, there's another man, I think, and he looks just like the man with the whip, except that his eyes are different. This is the man she truly loves and he's running through the forest as fast as he can.

The horse! Karl said. Come on with the horse before I freeze my nuts off.

But why a horse? Ben asked.

Why a horse?! Karl exclaimed. Because we've *got* a horse—that's why.

Sure, my father said. Do the best with what you've got and leave the rest to God. That's what I say.

My philosopher, my mother said, then kissed my father, laughed, reached inside her coat, pulled out a pistol, and fired it at the sky.

Come on and get me, you dirty varmints! she cried out.

I hugged her hard. I've got you! I shouted.

My little baby Joey, she whispered. My angel boy. Don't ever let them hurt you. Promise me, all right?

I promise, I said.

My mother was the most beautiful woman in the world when she got like this—going from hot to cold, from anger to love to sadness and back again. She kissed the top of my head and put the gun away, and I saw the two of us riding around the lake in a sleigh, blocks of ice stacked behind our seat. I saw Ben standing on the lake, making a movie of us the way he did every year at this time.

I had never seen the movie he had been making of me and my mother because he kept it on a single roll of film he had not yet processed. In that way, he explained, when we played the film back someday, it would be like a stop-action sequence from a George Méliès movie where my entire life would pass before your eyes as if it were taking place in only a few minutes.

In the first shot Ben ever took, I was ten days old, and I was asleep on my mother's lap, wrapped in a blanket, the two of us riding toward the far end of the lake, where willows and silver maple crowded the bank. Then, as the sleigh turned and came back toward the camera, I was awake on her lap, and I was one year old, and as I went by the camera I was two years old and sitting upright, holding the horse's reins.

Each time the picture changed I was a year older and yet, even though eleven years had now passed, Ben said the images would make you believe that time itself had vanished from the world—that my mother and I were making a single journey around a lake on a single winter afternoon.

Ah Joey, my beautiful Joey, my mother said. Then you're really my son?

Yes.

You mean I actually gave birth to you?

Yes.

She shook her head from side to side. Unbelievable! she said. She held me away from her. Such a sweet nose, she said.

She tugged once on each of my ears, then lifted my cap and roughed my hair. What a waste, what a waste. Maybe your father's right—that you should have been a girl.

Shh, Ben said. He's a boy, not a girl. Leave him be.

Hurry! Karl said. We gotta hurry. Look! Karl pointed to the far end of the lake where, behind the northern range of low, rolling hills, a wide, black wall of clouds rose up like a mountain. The clouds moved toward us as if the ocean were behind them, pushing them through the sky.

The Leskos pulled chisels from their overcoats, knelt down and started chopping and hammering along the narrow furrows they had made with their ice-marker. Karl slapped his shoulders and walked in circles around the fire, first one way, and then the other. This is why we're moving to California, he said. All right? Everyone else is out there already. Griffith's making features he's gonna charge two bucks a seat for—two bucks, can you believe it?—and I'm still pissing my life away on these two-reelers.

I was in California once, my father said. He walked alongside Karl, imitating Karl's every movement, slapping his hands against his shoulders whenever Karl did. I played with a band on a ship that went through the Panama Canal, from New York to San Francisco, my father said. I had the time of my life. I fell in love with the Osder girls. They were twins and I fell in love with both of them. Their family invented Osder powder, for removing unwanted facial hair. Their father kept the secret formula in a box, under his pillow.

In California we can make movies every day of the year without freezing our tushes off, Karl said. In California, Edison and his thugs won't burn down our studio and break our cameras. I got a letter from Zukor, you know—I got a letter from him, saying we should work together.

Ben cupped his palm over his eyes. Joey? he asked.

I see a horse falling through the ice, I said. The woman and the child are holding on to the horse and two men who look the same are trying to pull them from the ice. And there's blood. I see lots of blood, and it's turning the water black.

Terrific, Karl said. Love, danger, violence, rescue—we stick to the basics. That's terrific, Joey. Really terrific. I knew I could count on you. So okay. So one of you geniuses tell me— where do we start?

Inside the ice house, my mother said.

Why the ice house? Karl asked.

So we can get warm, my mother laughed. Then she started running across the ice, taking long strides, gliding and making believe her boots were ice skates. She jumped over the open runway, stopped, took out her pistol again, spun the chamber. She was having one of her wild days, when you never knew what she would do next. She turned toward us and shouted, as if she were leading a cavalry charge: Ready or not, here we come—The American Sun and Wind Moving Picture Company!

Then she fired the gun into the air, three times, and the explosions blasted through my skull like the sound the ice-covered lake would make if it were splitting open. I heard a man scream. The Leskos were trying to control their horse, which was hammering at the air with its hooves. The screaming came from the hilltop where I had been standing a few minutes before. A man stood there now, his hands clasped above his heart.

Holy mackerel! my mother said. I finally did it.

Ben! Karl yelled. Start shooting—we can figure out the story later. Hurry, Ben. Camera! Camera!

Ben did what Karl told him to do.

The man on the hill, hands pressed to his heart as if he'd been struck by a bullet, twirled in a circle, tumbled down the slope, rolling this way and that so that I was frightened his head would smash against boulders and tree trunks.

It's Izzie, my father shouted, clapping his hands. It's Izzie! I watched Izzie carom off a rock, sail onto the ice and spin around, face down. He lay there for a few seconds, as if dead, and I ran toward him.

When I was no more than ten feet away, he stood up, grinned, doffed his cap, and bowed.

Hurray for Izzie! I yelled.

Izzie was my mother's cousin, our stunt man when he was sober, and often when he was not. He could walk on the ledges of high buildings, stand on the wings of flying airplanes, jump out of burning buildings, and ride wild horses. He could duel with swords, drive cars like a maniac, and fight with his fists like Battling Levinsky.

How's my favorite little guy? he asked, and before I could answer, he hoisted me into the air and raced across the ice with me. I stretched my legs and arms way out, as if I were an airplane. We zoomed in for a landing, and he set me down beside the fire and started kissing my mother.

My father grabbed Izzie and began waltzing him around in circles, singing "The Beautiful Blue Danube."

Karl was screaming through his megaphone that time was money, that we were robbing him blind, that by the time we finished shooting in the ice house and got back out here, we'd have lost our light.

Easy does it, cousin, Izzie said, his arm around Karl's shoulder. Like I always say, the main thing in life is to have a good time and not to get hurt. Everything else is extra.

Not to get hurt? Karl said. Ha! I think maybe what we got here is a major case of the pot calling the kettle black.

I never risk injury, Izzie said, and he repeated words he gave to people when they told him he took too many chances: Everything I do in this life is figured out exactly.

The Leskos put away their chisels. One of them took a pair of ice tongs from the leather harness on the side of the horse, opened the tongs wide, and hooked them into a cake of ice.

Izzie rubbed his hands together. So what are we waiting for? he asked. Let's put this show on the road.

But what if it rains or it snows? my father asked. We have to think about that also. What if there's a storm? What do we do then?

We shoot our moving picture, Karl said, whether it rains or whether it snows or whether it storms or whether it stinks.

My father lifted his accordion, shrugged the straps into place over his shoulders, began playing "My Bonnie Lies Over the Ocean." My mother reached into the small telescope bag in which she kept her makeup, took out her mirror, passed a gold tube back and forth through the flames, to thaw it, then lifted the lid and twisted the tube of red lipstick upwards. She stacked my father's suitcases to eye level, set a mirror on top, and began doing her lips.

I saw fountains of blood explode from the bottom of the lake. The wind was roaring through the water like thunder, tearing holes in whatever was in its way—rocks, animals, trees, children—and I closed my eyes the way I did when I wanted a scene to change, and I saw that below the ice, water, and mud, an entire lost world existed—cities, buildings, castles, people—and that it was from this world that the blood was rising.

Here, sweetheart, my mother said. It's time. She handed me the mirror and lipstick so that, for our story, I could begin to make myself into her daughter.

I looked at my image in the mirror—stared through the dark holes in the middle of my eyes and imagined that on the wall at the back of my skull, my face, like the pictures inside Ben's camera, was upside down.

So tell me, Joey, Izzie asked. Would you like to be our director?

Sure, I said.

He handed me Karl's megaphone. Taped to the wide end of the funnel was a circle of cardboard, and in the middle of the cardboard Karl had cut out a rectangle, so his megaphone could double as a viewfinder. I looked through the viewfinder, squinting until the only thing I could see were my mother's lips. They were wine-red and moist and someday soon in theaters in New York City they would fill entire screens, forty feet wide and thirty feet high.

The boy wants to be the director, Izzie said.

Fine with me, Karl said. I had enough already for a lifetime. Take over. He got my blessing.

Good. So here's everything you need to know, Izzie said. Are you ready?

Ready, I said.

Okay. Then repeat after me—*Camera*.

Camera!

Action.

Action!

Cut.

Cut!

Now you know everything Karl knows, Izzie said, and he kissed me hard on the mouth. Now you're a director.

The Leskos were floating cakes of ice along the runway, toward shore. I held up a thin strip of black velvet, next to the camera. When my mother turned and looked at it, her pupils dilated and her pale blue eyes went dark.

Cut, Karl said, and Ben stopped shooting. My mother looked away. I put the strip of velvet in my pocket, and while Ben counted, I back-cranked the camera for him, eight turns. Then he tilted the camera down, its lens pointed at the open water, and he cranked the handle forward, so that before one scene ended the next scene would begin. That way, my mother's eyes would seem to dissolve in the dark water of the lake. You would see her face, aflame with fear, and then you would see her eyes grow dark with despair, after which the scene would melt, and you would move right through my mother's eyes until you were staring into water as deep and black as a starless night.

One of the Leskos hooked a cake of ice with a pike pole, dragged the cake onto a plank. When there were six cakes of ice lined up, they jammed them together, shoved a slab of wood into them at one end—there were two metal spikes in the wood—attached the slab of wood to the horse with rope and made the horse pull the blocks of ice along the plank, to shore.

Ben raised his camera slowly, set it in position, and photographed the northern crescent of the lake, where Mister

Lesko was walking behind his horse, plowing the ice. Mister Lesko played my mother's cruel husband. Mister Lesko's son played The Gentle Stranger.

Because of the different coats they now wore, I could tell who was the father and who was the son. The father wore the beaver coat and the hat with earlaps. The son wore a ragged brown wool coat Izzie had given him from our costume chest. The son worked without a hat, so that the winter light, playing through his brown curls from behind, made him appear young and kind.

I wore a wig made of long auburn tresses, and under my black coat, I now had on a white blouse and a soiled blue pinafore.

Action! Karl called out, the megaphone to his mouth.

Mister Lesko stopped plowing, took out his whip, raised it above his shoulder.

Camera! Karl called.

Ben began cranking, and Mister Lesko started whipping his horse.

No! I screamed. I shot out from where I stood, streaked across the ice, and grabbed at his arm. He threw me off easily.

Cut! Karl shouted.

Wonderful, Joey, he said. That was wonderful. I didn't expect you to do that.

I had not expected to do it either, but I didn't say so.

Izzie took the whip from Mister Lesko's hand, raised it high in the air, as if to strike him. Instead, he pivoted and lashed out at the horse. The whip cracked, making a sound like a bullet firing, and at the sound, the horse bolted forward.

The lash never touched the horse's flank.

Like that, Izzie said. You do it like that or you let me wear your clothes and do it for you. If you whip the horse again, I'll whip you. Got it? And you *never* touch the boy.

My mother stroked my hair, and I leaned back against her bosom. She always loved me more when I was her daughter than when I was her son. At home, cleaning the house, cooking our meals, or doing the wash, my mother was as calm as any mother in the world. When we were out doing errands, and people told her they'd seen her in moving pictures, she would blush and look away, like the bashful young maidens she sometimes played. Yet when we actually started making a picture, she lived in the story and characters as if they were more real than the rest of her life.

Listen to me, she said. You'll run away and get help. I'll send you to town for provisions. He won't suspect.

Izzie squatted and dipped his hand in the water, testing its coldness.

Mister Lesko coiled the end of his whip.

My father took out a small pair of scissors and snipped the fingers from a pair of wool gloves and let them fall to the ice. That way, the pink tips of his fingers exposed, he could continue to play his instruments.

Behind the clouds, the light in the sky was starting to fade, and I was frightened that we would run out of time to make this year's moving picture of me and my mother. I wanted to ask my mother if she were frightened too—if she too feared that if we ever missed a year, our lives, like the film of our lives, might end. I imagined sitting with my mother on a ledge of ice after everyone else was gone, above the open channel. I imagined us slipping quietly over the edge, descending noiselessly through the water.

I had given them one story and now I invented another, about how my mother and I slipped through the lake's sandy bottom and made our way into the lost world below, so that we might find out the source of the howling and the blood.

Ben photographed Mister Lesko's eyes, and then he photographed the horse's eyes. Next he photographed Mister Lesko's son, who, with tongs, was hefting blocks of ice from the plank onto the sleigh. When Mister Lesko's son looked at his father, his eyes became soft, like the eyes of a wounded dog.

Brilliant, Karl said to Ben, peering through his viewfinder. You're a genius, Joey, to have thought of making the husband and the lover the same man.

Their faces are the same, but their eyes are opposite, Ben said.

Yes, Karl said, and his voice was soft now too. You can make miracles with eyes, Ben—I gotta hand that to you. In life, you see, eyes are just little things in a face, with skin that goes up and down over them, but in moving pictures, the eyes—oh the eyes are everything.

A woman in a long black coat, a black babushka on her head, was walking across the ice, a line of six children follow-ing her like ducklings. Two of the children carried wood and sticks. The other four carried large round stones. The woman bore a yoke across her shoulders, square wooden boxes sus-pended from each end.

Mister Lesko's son lifted the yoke from the woman's shoulder, kissed her once on each cheek. The children wore black hats with earlaps. They arranged the stones around the wood, and set about making a fire.

The woman removed Mister Lesko's gloves and pried open his hands, one finger at a time. She took off her own gloves and smeared Mister Lesko's fingers with what ap-peared to be goose fat. Mister Lesko closed his eyes, opened his mouth and howled, but without sound.

The children stared at Mister Lesko's hands as if they were watching a hunter's trap being forced open. They formed a circle around him to shield him from the wind. Mister Les-ko's son removed pots of food from the boxes that hung from the yoke, and set the pots upon a grate above the fire. When the food was ready, the children fed Mister Lesko by dipping metal cups into the pot and raising the cups to his lips.

When Mister Lesko was finished eating, he made the sign of the cross above each child. He pointed to the food. Then the children reached in with their cups and scooped out portions for themselves. The woman smeared a long strip of cloth with fat, and wound the cloth around Mister Lesko's hands. She pulled his gloves on over the bandages, as if stretching them onto wooden forms. I imagined that his hands were in the flames, that I could smell the sweet fragrance of singed wool.

When people froze, I knew, they sank to the bottom of lakes, but when water froze, it rose to the top. If this were not true, Ben taught me—if the world were so created that when water froze, it contracted and became heavier, all the creatures and plants that lived in the lake would be crushed by the weight of the ice, and when spring came, everything in this lake, and in all the iced-over rivers, streams, and oceans of the world, would be dead.

The children stamped out the fire with their boots. Mister Lesko's son put the pots back in the boxes, fixed the yoke across the woman's shoulders, and attached the boxes to the ends of the yoke.

Mister Lesko gestured to the children. They came near to him and he kissed each of them on the forehead, after which they turned, faced us directly, and waited. The light, coming from behind them, turned their faces black, however, and I could not tell which were boys or which were girls. They stood still until the woman joined them, whereupon they bowed their heads to us, in unison.

Then the children lifted the large stones and walked back across the ice behind the woman, in single file, the stones pressed to their stomachs.

Mister Lesko's son closed his father's fingers around the handles of the ice plow.

Ben unscrewed his camera from the tripod and wrapped it in a blanket. I helped load the sleds with our equipment and we moved back across the ice again, up onto land, through the snow, to the ice house.

Our story was simple, and we made it up as we went along the way we always did.

My mother was living a harsh and lonely life, married to Mister Lesko and caring for me, her beloved daughter. In early scenes, which we would shoot back at our studio the next day and patch in later, you would see the two of us slaving away for Mister Lesko in his kitchen, and submitting to his tyranny, until the day upon which The Gentle Stranger wandered into our world.

The Gentle Stranger owned a book of poems, and in the evenings, when our chores were done, he would read to us from Tennyson, Swinburne, and Shelley. Karl liked to put sections of poems into the titles because if the pictures didn't tell people what to feel, he said, the words would.

Ben disagreed. He believed our stories should be told in pictures only, so that anyone in the world, in any time and place, could understand them. Because all the stories I made up came to me in a series of pictures that marched across the screen inside my head—pictures that became less real the instant I even tried to describe them—I agreed with Ben.

We think in pictures, Ben always said. Not words.

Even though I agreed with him, whenever I found pictures and people in my head I wanted to save, I gave them names, the way I named The Gentle Stranger. And I invented titles to put on the doors and windows of their rooms, so that someday I would be able to find them again.

THE GENTLE STRANGER FINDS A NEW HOME WITH THE MOTHER AND HER LOVE-CHILD

In exchange for food and lodging, The Gentle Stranger worked for Mister Lesko, cutting wood and harvesting ice. Mister Lesko let him use the ice house for a home and he slept there at night, wrapped in old blankets, between walls of ice and sawdust.

Then one night, after Mister Lesko got drunk and fell asleep, we stole away to the ice house, and my mother told The Gentle Stranger our story: how she had been sent to work for Mister Lesko as a housekeeper, and how Mister Lesko had forced himself upon her, after which, in her shame, she had had no choice but to become his wife.

Perhaps it was God's will, my mother said, drawing me close to her. For had I not submitted to Mister Lesko, my most precious jewel would not be here.

That was when The Gentle Stranger declared his love for my mother. He went down on his knees and clasped my mother's hands.

I have never loved another as I love you, he said. You have rescued me from the dead. Without you I cannot live.

My mother's true heart showed in her eyes, but she pulled her hands free and turned away.

I am a married woman, she said.

I looked at The Gentle Stranger and I looked at my mother. I took his hand and I took hers—the hand upon which she wore her wedding band—and I joined their hands together.

Then we argued.

Karl said my mother and The Gentle Stranger should now plan to murder Mister Lesko—to arrange for an accident, where he drowned in the lake.

My father said that the three of us should just run away together and start a new life. Let love reign triumphant! he said.

Oh Simon, my mother said, and she rested her head on my father's shoulder. You are the dearest man in the world, aren't you?

I like happy endings that make me cry, my father said.

Izzie said the problem was that we didn't know who The Gentle Stranger was and where he came from and why he was there and why and how he had been saved from the dead. If they killed Mister Lesko, they'd get caught and go to jail and I'd be an orphan. Why, he asked, should people pay good money to see lives more miserable than their own?

Izzie's right, my father said.

I said that maybe The Gentle Stranger had originally come to the lake intending to commit suicide. When he looked into the water he had seen, not his own reflection, but that of my mother, and seeing her eyes, he had decided to live.

Ben beamed, and said we could start with the scene in the ice house—of them holding hands—and then go to a dream-like flashback by using a piece of fine gauze over the lens, of The Gentle Stranger staring at my mother's image in the water—her fingers clasped together in prayer, her hands themselves seeming to dissolve, only to reappear and rise up, as if disembodied, from the depths of the lake.

In addition to which, Izzie said, who would ever believe a square hole in an ice-covered lake was natural? Everyone would think we were tricking them with miniatures and shots we cooked up in the studio.

Karl said the story was getting too complicated, and too expensive. He asked my opinion, and I suggested we combine the two stories—The Gentle Stranger and my mother could still plot to kill Mister Lesko—but because they were incapable of such an act, they could also change their minds at the last minute.

And then, Karl said, just when they change their minds— I got it, I got it!—there can be a terrible accident that kills Mister Lesko anyway.

Except that, because they planned the murder, I said, nobody will believe it was an accident, and they'll be made to suffer forever for what they did *not* do.

Because we were going to shoot indoors, Ben changed to the longest of his three lenses, and set the aperture wide open. To crank the right number of turns—sixteen frames per second was the usual rate—Ben hummed to himself while he shot. His favorite, because it had such a steady beat, eight frames per turn, was "The Anvil Chorus" from *Il Trovatore*. But he used different songs for different speeds, and if my father played too slowly or too fast, all Ben had to do was give him a look and my father would change the tempo.

Because the action and movement you thought you saw on the screen took place inside you—there were no real moving pictures, only a series of photos you put together inside your mind—the fewer photos there were per second the faster people on the screen seemed to move, and the more photos there were per second the slower they moved. When Karl wanted people to move more quickly, Ben undercranked—and if he wanted them to move more slowly, he overcranked.

To make use of the available light, we kept the door of the ice house wide open, and set up a clothesline between two trees, a stiff white bedsheet hanging from it to reflect light into the house. Later, Karl said, we would tint this part of the film blue, to transform it into night.

Ben could mix wonderful colors—gold for dawn, yellow for candlelight, red for fires or war scenes, peach-glow for sunsets—and sometimes, late at night in the old trolley barn we had converted into our studio and home, he would let me bathe the strips of film in dyes, and choose the colors we would use, not just to indicate the time of day, as now, or to emphasize what was happening—the way we did for battles and weddings—but to create an atmosphere that helped you understand the *feelings* in the scenes: pale blue for sadness, glowing ambers for peacefulness, crimson for passion, ruby reds for lust, forest greens for happiness.

But the colors for feelings—unlike the colors for night, dawn, fire, sunsets, and candlelight—were never fixed. Sometimes forest green could show how happy our people were, while at other times it could reveal fear. Sometimes bathing a scene in indigo or sapphire could let you sense the joy our characters were experiencing, and sometimes it helped you to feel that the actors and actresses were merely, like the color itself, blue.

As soon as Karl had arranged the scene the way he wanted, my mother wrapped me in a cloak, and gave me a basket of food, a letter placed at the bottom of the basket, to take to The Gentle Stranger, who was now hiding in the forest, waiting for us.

But if you meet in the forest, how would the accident take place on the lake? Karl asked.

Okay, Izzie said. This is how it works. We cut through the rope, so when he's chasing them through the forest with his horse and sleigh, the rope snaps, the sleigh throws him off flying, and he goes tumbling down the hill into the water.

But we have to figure out how it becomes an accident instead of murder, Karl said.

Maybe it's the opposite of the Red Sea, my father said. Maybe the lake closes shut with ice, and then it opens again and he falls in, splash!

Good, Simon, Izzie said. So we chop out a chunk of ice and tow it in, and then we tow it back out. You can show me floating in the lake, face down, in Mister Lesko's coat and his hat, like I'm drowned, and then the child pokes me with the pike pole, and turns me over and I'll give you a look from under water that will make people freeze in their seats.

You know what people will call you, dressed like that, in Mister Lesko's hat? my father asked Izzie.

No. What will people call me, dressed like that?

A schmuck with earlaps, my father said.

Izzie began smearing his arms and legs with grease, for when he would be drowning in the lake, and while he did I remembered the first picture I had seen in my head, of a woman drowning, only I didn't understand how that was to come true anymore since we had changed things and decided that Mister Lesko would be the one to drown.

As soon as Mister Lesko found my mother's letter to The Gentle Stranger and read it, he took out his whip. My mother crawled backwards, across the snow, to the ice house, her forearm across her eyes. Mister Lesko's arm came flashing down and I leapt in front of my mother, covering her body with my own. The whip's lash cut into my cheek, and the burning sensation—warm and liquid—felt wonderful.

I had not known this would happen.

Before my mother could tend to me, Izzie lifted Mister Lesko from the ground and was pounding him against the side of the ice house. Mister Lesko's son lifted a pike pole and tried to stab Izzie, but Izzie saw him coming and stepped aside.

The pike pole rammed into Mister Lesko's side.

Keep shooting, Karl said. We'll cut it all up later.

They're cut up now, my father said. He put down his accordion and packed handfuls of snow onto the side of my face.

Izzie reached inside his coat, pulled out a leather-covered flask, and took a long drink. He shouldn't drink while he works, my father said.

Don't drink while you work, my mother said.

If I need a wife, I'll buy one, Izzie said.

Izzie drank again, touched my head gently, and when I saw his eyes go moist, I imagined he was thinking of his own wife, Flora, a Ziegfeld girl who had left him two years before and had run off with a trombone player.

My mother grabbed Karl's arm. Don't let him work when he drinks, she said. Please.

Just look at his eyes, would you?! Karl said. Look at the rage in them. How wonderful!

Falling into the lake will sober him up, my father said. Everything Izzie does is figured out exactly.

We moved to the top of the hill, and Ben set up his camera there—first to show us racing through the forest to warn The Gentle Stranger that Mister Lesko was coming to do him harm, and then to show Mister Lesko charging through the forest with his horse and sleigh.

Below us, one of the Leskos had an arm around the other's waist, helping him toward shore.

We photographed my mother sawing through the horse's reins with a kitchen knife.

We photographed us changing our minds, and trying to tie the reins back together, but before we could, Mister Lesko, believing we were trying to escape, beat us away with his whip.

So we fled into the forest, past Ben's camera, and it felt wonderful to run across the frozen ground, holding tight to my mother's hand, the frigid air kissing my cheek, sealing the blood there. Izzie was on the ice now, where Mister Lesko was tying the horse's reins back together. He pushed Mister Lesko out of the sleigh. Mister Lesko tried to stop him, but Izzie knocked him to the ground with the back of his hand,

and took the horse and sleigh. He rode to a point fifty yards away, then turned back.

Ben photographed me and my mother slipping down the hill, hand in hand, to the lake. The Gentle Stranger stood in the middle of the lake, waiting for us, but where our camera had been, jagged slabs of ice now floated like small islands. Our plan was to jump from island to island toward the south end of the lake where there was a waterfall.

Ben could photograph us from the other side of the waterfall and, although we would be nowhere near the waterfall, he could foreshorten the distance to make it appear we were in danger of plunging over, to our death.

Ben photographed Izzie, disguised as Mister Lesko, speeding across the snow in the sleigh. Then he moved his camera back onto the ice and photographed me and my mother running along the shore until we found a place where we could step out onto the ice. The fire on the lake was gone and Ben said we had to hurry, for the cold air might cause flashes of static electricity inside the camera.

My mother and I set out across the lake, and we called to The Gentle Stranger.

Izzie started down the hill. I saw that the real Mister Lesko was smiling, and I called out to Izzie to be careful. The reins! I called. The reins!

It doesn't matter, my father said. You heard Karl. Whether it rains or it snows or it stinks, we shoot.

But it was too late. The reins snapped. The horse buckled as if its forelegs had been chopped off. It tumbled downhill, crashed into a tree, rolled over and kept rolling. The sleigh skidded on a single runner in an opposite direction. Izzie leapt out, but he had not planned to do so at that spot, and though he avoided crashing into a tree, he landed hard, shoulder first, against a boulder, and spun upside down, in a somersault. He clutched at his shoulder.

Wonderful! Karl called out through his megaphone.

My father pulled at the rope that was hooked into the slab of ice we were riding on, so that at the exact moment when the horse reached the shore, the ice moved, and the horse fell directly into the water, its head cracking against the ice's edge.

I heard a sound come from its neck, like that of a tree snapping in high wind.

In the open water, blood pooled.

Izzie rolled into the water behind the horse.

Mister Lesko stopped smiling. He held to his side, where Izzie had rammed the pike pole, as if it were only now that he felt the pain. His horse thrashed at the water, trying to climb out, and the more wildly it thrashed, the more the blood in the water foamed.

My mother watched Izzie raise his hand, grasping at air, then sink beneath the water's bubbling skin. Her eyes rolled up in their sockets. She fainted, and lay across our island of ice, one leg caught under her, her hair trailing in the water.

The Gentle Stranger came toward us, leaping from island to island, as if to rescue me and my mother, but when he got to us, he plunged past, straight into the water, and grabbed for the horse's reins.

From the shore, Mister Lesko waded into the lake.

Where's Izzie? my father asked. He cupped his hands around his mouth, and called out: *Izzie! Oh, Izzie!* Where *are* you?

The horse twitched, floated up and rolled to its side.

Then Izzie rose to the surface. Shit, he said. It's colder than a pair of witch's tits down there.

Suddenly, the horse rose up from the water, above Izzie, as if it were about to fly.

The horse! I cried. *The horse!*

Izzie turned, but too late, and the horse dropped down upon him with its full weight. Izzie disappeared beneath the horse and the water. The horse had one hoof on our island of ice, but the hoof slipped and the horse fell backwards, its neck catching on a point of the ice, the ice tearing out a long gash and stripping the skin away. As if sprung from a trap, a splintered bone shot through the exposed flesh.

Mister Lesko waded through the water as if he were walking through brambles.

We have to save them, Ben said.

Keep shooting, Karl said. Don't stop.

But they could die, Ben said. This is really happening.

Luck! Karl said. Sometimes, after you give up all hope, and when you least expect it, you get lucky. Go figure.

Izzie appeared behind us, climbed onto our island. I think the horse is dead, he said.

See? Karl said. When it comes to stunts, Izzie never takes chances. Keep shooting, Ben. Only leave Mister Lesko out of the frame. We can't have two husbands show up in the same scene.

My mother opened her eyes. You're alive, she said to me. You're alive!

My mother stood. And you too, she said to Izzie, but when she went to embrace him, Mister Lesko, struggling in water where he could no longer stand, snatched at her ankle.

My mother tumbled over the island's edge, into the water.

Wonderful! Karl said.

This wasn't supposed to happen, my father said.

Yes it was, Karl said. Don't you remember what Joey said about seeing a woman drowning, about the woman and the child holding to the horse, about the horse in the water.

Ah! my father said. You're right again.

So I dove into the water to rescue my mother. I saw her dark hair floating through the blood, and I reached out, closed my hands around the hair, but at that instant the horse rolled up between us, as if it were a huge barrel, and I found myself holding to its blood-drenched mane.

Mister Lesko's son was on the shore now, tying a rope to the reins, and pulling. I turned and saw pink water drip from the corner of my mother's mouth. Her eyelids moved up, globes of milk-white gelatin like those we set before the projector's lens, rolling where her eyes had been.

I felt as if my chest were being crushed between walls of thick limestone. Mister Lesko and his son pulled steadily on the rope, to haul their horse from the water.

My mother's mouth was open, and her lips were white.

In the camera, I knew, black was white and white was black. In my mother's telescope bag, there would still be a perfect red impression of her mouth on tissue, where she had blotted it.

The storm is here, my father said, pointing to the sky.

We have to help them, Ben said. They'll get frostbite. They'll lose their toes, their fingers.

Keep shooting, Karl said. It's even better than what the boy saw. It's real.

Ben left the camera, grabbed blankets from the ground— the blankets in which he kept his spools of film and his extra lenses—and he rushed toward us.

Make a fire, he said to my father. Make a fire. Quickly.

Karl took Ben's place and cranked the camera's handle.

If we don't use it now, we'll use it later, he said. Nothing is wasted. Nothing is lost.

I climbed out of the water. My teeth were clicking like dice. Ben wrapped me in a blanket, and began rubbing my cheeks with his hands.

You have the heart of a murderer, Ben said to Karl.

Don't make me laugh, Karl said. Did I cut the reins? Did I push them into the water? Did I kill the horse?

Izzie emerged from the water, my mother in his arms. He set her down on the snow, covered her with blankets, put a flask of whiskey to her lips.

The horse lay on its side, blood spilling from its mouth as if a long strip of red film were unfurling from its innards.

Mister Lesko pried open the horse's teeth and blood shot out onto his face as if pumped from a fire hose.

The horse twitched, pawed the air with its hooves.

Suddenly, my mother stood up, as if she were neither wet, nor cold, nor frightened. She reached into her coat and took out her pistol.

She went to the horse, put the muzzle of the pistol to its forehead, and fired twice.

Mister Lesko and his son went down on their knees. They each made the sign of the cross. Above us, dark clouds were lower than the hills, separating and spreading now as if, like thin, soiled cloth, the sky itself were rotting.

Mister Lesko bent his head, pressed it against the horse's neck, and wept.

Cut! Karl said. Cut! We got it.

1918

We sat in the projection room, watching French, American, and German soldiers die, while on screen Mister Griffith, in a pith helmet, walked among them. Miss Gish and Billy Bitzer, Mister Griffith's cameraman, sat behind me with my mother and father.

Miss Gish's skin was the fairest I had ever seen, and her almond eyes were even larger than my mother's. Her auburn hair was braided and tied in a brown taffeta schoolgirl's bow, and there was something in the hollows of her narrow cheeks that made her appear lost—as if, I thought, she were intending to play an orphan a lonely couple might choose to adopt as their ward. Below her blue wool frock coat, which she left unbuttoned, she wore a brown pin-check gingham dress.

Mister Griffith sat to one side of me, my father to the other.

Behind me, Miss Gish whispered to my mother that she had it on good authority—a distinguished French dramatist who was herself the mysterious woman allowed to visit Captain Dreyfus on Devil's Island—that Chinese men were the best lovers because Chinese women were so difficult to arouse. Miss Gish told my mother that Mister Griffith insisted it be written into her contract, as well as the contract of her sister Dorothy, that in their films no man ever be allowed to kiss either of them upon the lips.

Mister Griffith turned and, his hand upon my thigh for balance, and breathing Izzie's sour mash whiskey into my face, he talked of rolling barrages, soul-sickening smells, and shell-scorched orchards, of having looked out from trenches across no–man's–land at the desolation of nothingness.

We watched a group of French soldiers dig a trench. On the screen, Mister Griffith mimed their digging motions, then stumbled into their dugout and emerged, hat in hand, and signaled "Cut!" to the cameraman.

We laughed, but Mister Griffith declared that he was never too proud to show unedited footage. He spoke of air attacks on London by dirigibles, and described how, after a night raid, wherein a bomb had demolished a tram, the cries of the wounded rose from the street and soaked the air. We saw dead horses and a slender finger of stone that rose from the rubble of what had once been a cathedral.

Mister Griffith appeared within the ruin, dressed in a tweed suit, a bow tie, and a tin hat. He smiled from the screen as if welcoming us to a picture palace.

Promoters boast of having made motion pictures for which the settings and actors cost a million dollars, he said. But the settings of my new moving picture — the one for which I seek your collaboration — will cost untold sums. For I will use nothing less than the most expensive settings that have ever been utilized in the making of movies.

With his left hand he gestured to Ben to change reels, while with his right hand he caressed my thigh, then let his hand fall between my legs, into the folds of my wedding dress.

I pushed his hand away and grabbed my father's arm.

War's hell, son, my father said.

So's this movie, Izzie said.

Until this moment, Mister Griffith stated, we have merely seen the actual war. Now we will see its true drama. For I am not, you see, interested in history alone, but in something more eternal—in the history of feelings!

On the screen, an American soldier was dying. The American soldier wore blackface in the way white actors had worn blackface when playing Negroes in *The Birth of a Nation*.

The Negro soldier has found himself in the same shell hole with a white Southern officer, Mister Griffith explained. When the officer was hit, it was the Negro soldier who rescued him and, in so doing, was himself mortally wounded.

The officer was played by Bobby Harron, and though his face was splattered with mud, he looked very handsome.

Bobby Harron put a canteen of water to the Negro soldier's lips, but the Negro pushed away the canteen, and sat up wide-eyed. Mammy! Mammy! he cried out.

The officer removed his helmet, cradled the Negro in his arms and pretended to be the Negro's mother.

The officer rocked the Negro soldier in his arms as if he were rocking his own child to sleep.

Then the officer bent down and kissed the Negro soldier full on the lips.

Is it not a dramatic and touching moment? Mister Griffith asked.

He doesn't really know what he's doing, Izzie whispered.

The camera opens and shuts, opens and shuts with equal time, Mister Griffith said. So half of everything you do is never seen. Take away the sound, and you lose half of your half, you see, thereby leaving upon the screen a mere quarter of what you have achieved. That is why expression must be four times as deep and true as it would normally be.

On the screen, the officer's lips remained pressed against the lips of the Negro. The expression on the Negro's face, as the officer withdrew from their kiss, was blissful.

Mister Griffith's mouth was close to my ear, telling me that on my wedding night I must not let an innocent groom into a garden that had not been well prepared.

Kindly keep your hands to yourself, Mister Griffith, Miss Gish said, speaking to him as if she were his schoolmistress.

Christ, Wark, Mister Bitzer said. Lay off. It's a *guy*.

Mister Griffith's hand left my thigh, but I hardly noticed, so strong within me was the image of the white man kissing the Negro.

For a boy, if truly you be one, he said to me, you make the most wonderful girl.

While Mister Griffith continued to talk to us of what he had seen of the War, I dreamt of lying in the Holy Cross cemetery at night, under a chestnut tree, the sweet fragrance of decaying leaves about me.

If I could prepare the chestnuts the way I wanted to, I believed I could get the boys at school to stop mocking me. And if I could make up a new story every week, one that Ben and I might turn into a moving picture—even if these stories became moving pictures nobody ever saw—I could keep him from being sad so much of the time, for ever since my Uncle Karl had moved to California and my mother had stopped making movies, joy had disappeared from his life.

Viewed as drama, Mister Griffith declared, the War was in most ways disappointing, you see, and that is why I have come here today to solicit your collaboration.

Listen, Izzie said. Stop crapping us, okay, Wark? You're here because we got what you want—the film—and because you got something we want.

The money, my father stated.

You said it, Simon.

I did, my father said. Because money can't buy happiness, although it certainly helps when you're miserable.

Will you fly the plane for me, then, my good man, Mister Griffith asked Izzie, so that we might add to the actual footage of the War the high drama it has heretofore lacked?

Sure, Izzie said. If you pay my price, you cheap old Jew.

I am not a dreamer, Mister Griffith stated. Whatever I

imagine and see inside my head, I can create upon the screen. There is *nothing*, you see—no feeling, person, or event in all of history—that I cannot render.

How sad, Ben said.

From his flask, Izzie poured whiskey into my mother's cup of tea. She lifted her veil and sipped.

My dearest Hannah, Mister Griffith said, inclining his head toward my mother. I have been among foreign women too long. I hope you will allow me, then, the pleasure of gazing once more upon your incomparably lovely face.

Leave her alone, Ben said. For God's sake, Wark!

My father knelt beside my mother. There's nothing to be ashamed of, dearest, he said. He reached out, to touch my mother's hair, but she slapped his hand away.

Don't you come *near* my face, she snapped.

If I could be in the cemetery when nobody else was there, I could gather the chestnuts and bring them home. I could leave them in my closet until they were hard as stone, drill holes through them, string them on shoelaces, and take them with me to school. Then, when the Italian boys searched my pockets for money, they would find the chestnuts and I would hold one of them out, dare them to smash it with one of theirs, and, as each of theirs split open, I would accumulate as mine all the victories theirs had previously acquired.

Mister Griffith moved near to my mother again, so that the brim of his fawn-colored Stetson touched her veil. He stared through the veil and seemed to understand for the first time that where there was once something, there was now nothing.

The way I look at it is this, my father said, his hand cupped to Mister Griffith's ear. Sometimes no nose is good nose.

My mother arched her ankle as if she were a ballet dancer, and for a moment I feared she might take off her shoe, to show Mister Griffith where two of her toes were missing. Instead, she scratched her ankle and lifted her cup toward Izzie, for more whiskey.

To tell the truth, she said, I was never the kind of girl who had her heart set on becoming Cinderella.

It could have been worse, my father explained to Mister Griffith. Mister Lesko and his son lost their legs. Now they sit at home like stumps.

Mister Griffith looked at my father with disdain. He opened his mouth, but no words came forth.

In my head, I wrote out a title for this day of my life:

D. W. GRIFFITH PAYS A VISIT TO

THE AMERICAN SUN & WIND MOVING PICTURE COMPANY
OCTOBER 15, 1918

Mister Griffith walked across the studio and, directly below the gallery Ben and I used for constructing our scenery, he stepped up onto the rolling platform that served as our camera stand. Covering his eyes with one hand, he thrust his other hand forward as if to shield himself from blinding light.

Now I see it all! he declared.

He uncovered his eyes, and walked into the set Ben had arranged—a painted backdrop of a room that contained only an iron bed, a kitchen chair, and a bureau upon which was fixed a large oval mirror.

When I looked into this mirror things were always reversed: When I was dressed as a boy, I saw a girl. When I was dressed as a girl, I saw a boy.

Mister Griffith spoke. You will be the Angel of Mercy, then, dear Hannah. Yes! Your face will be covered, as now, with a veil, for you will tend to the wounded and dying as they are carried from the trenches—you will ride with them in ambulances to the field hospitals. . . .

Please stop, Ben said. We told you before. Hannah no longer works in moving pictures.

And just as she will aid others in being reborn from the dead, Mister Griffith continued, so will she, as a great star, herself be reborn. When lightning splits the heavens and harsh rains fall, her shining face will appear to the French soldiers, even as Joan of Arc appeared to them in the mists above the trenches . . .

Mister Griffith came toward us, but I looked past him, to his reflection in the mirror, where he seemed not to be approaching us, but to be moving away.

I closed my eyes, and when I looked in the mirror again, Mister Griffith had passed from view, and I thought of how, as Ben had taught me, the greatest things in life were those things we could not see or touch—feelings, memories, love.

It's true about him being a Jew, though, Izzie explained. It's why he always wears hats with large brims. It's an old actor's trick—so you won't notice his big schnoz so much.

When President Wilson held a private screening for *Birth of a Nation*, Mister Griffith declared, our president said, and I quote, Why, it is like writing history with lightning, and my only regret is that it is all so terribly true!

I looked in the mirror and saw a young girl dressed, as I was, in a simple wedding dress. I imagined that the girl, asleep in the cemetery, was dreaming of her wedding night. I saw her young man walking along a country lane, his face, in the moonlight, bright with expectation. As he came to a curve in the road and started to climb the hill that led to the cemetery, an automobile bore down upon him, its single headlamp devouring him as if it were a giant eye.

I have made a most generous offer to your brother Karl, Mister Griffith told my mother. I have offered to buy the original negative so that I might, in the privacy of my own screening room, draw consolation from watching you adrift in the frozen pond.

The negative is not for sale, Ben said. We told you before.

If he can't buy it, he'll steal it, Izzie said. Wait and see if he don't. So listen. I'll make *you* a deal, Wark. I'll fly any plane you want—Kraut or Frog or even one of those lousy Limey cracker boxes—only you pay cash up front, on the barrelhead.

Yes, my mother said. The money first. Because love is sweet, as Poppa used to say, but tastes best with bread.

Izzie whispered to me that Flora was back, and had promised to fly with him again. Ben lifted the bride's veil from atop my tiara, let it fall across my face. He carried his camera to our set, began arranging the muslin light diffusers that operated on our overhead trolley system.

I stared at the oval mirror, made believe it was a window through which I was looking out at the sky, and I let myself float through that sky until I was high above the Hudson River, my arms spread wide. I wanted to be smaller than the smallest bird—to be gliding on warm, gentle currents of air. And then I wanted to be so small that I would be able to live inside Ben's camera, holding fast to the sprocket holes of the film as it looped from spool to spool.

Although Mister Griffith eyed me with severity, when he spoke to me, his voice was surprisingly gentle.

I have often thought what a grand invention it would be, dear child, he said, if someone were to make a magic box wherein we might store the precious moments of our lives. Then, later on, in dark hours, we could open this box and receive, for at least a few moments, a breath of its stored memory.

Using the bureau below the mirror for a desk, Mister Griffith wrote out a check and gave it to Izzie.

Long life and happiness to the young bride, Mister Griffith said then. As Virgil has written: *Optima quaque dies . . . prima fugit!* It is ever the brightest days of life that are the first to flee!

Mister Griffith turned to Izzie. What I had in mind, he said, is a moment when our hero, having used up his fuel in pursuit of the evil Hun, can escape death only by walking along the wing of his plane—while the plane itself remains in full flight—across a bridge of air, and onto the wing of another.

You got it, Izzie said.

But before that, we see the evil Hun's plane catch fire and plunge to the sea below.

I could do the falling leaf for that—a snap—only what

you do, Izzie said, is you cut the camera before I hit bottom, and I pull the plane out.

Through the webbed lace of my bride's veil, I watched Izzie and Mister Griffith plan their scenes, and while they did I thought of how, when the young woman lifted her veil and gazed at the mirror, Ben would know it was not only the woman and her young man I was seeing, but my mother, as she had looked until the day, now nearly three years past, when she had fallen into the lake and her toes, lips, and nose had turned black from frostbite.

You're a fool, Izzie said to Mister Griffith.

Yes I am, Mister Griffith said.

And a thief, Izzie said.

Yes I am, Mister Griffith said. But I steal from the best. All artists steal, you see. But if one steals from others—even from the Creator of the Universe Himself—one must know what to steal. One must know how to take the finest fruits and flowers of their gardens and make them grow in one's own.

I took my mother's hand, led her past our two small dressing rooms and along the corridor that lay between our apartment and Ben's room. My mother kept her eyes closed, as if she were a blind woman. In her blouse of sun-kissed linen and in my gown of ivory-white tulle, and with a black veil across her face and a white veil across mine, a stranger, seeing us approach, would surely have taken us for mother and daughter.

It was at that moment that I imagined the day upon which I would marry. And I could see that, the ceremony over, my mother was lifting her veil for the first time since she had fallen through the ice.

I lay in the cemetery, covered with leaves, gazing up at the starlit sky and remembering how Izzie's plane had dropped through the air, twirling like the falling leaf for which his stunt was named.

When I was a child my mother taught me that each time somebody you loved died, a new star formed in the heavens.

I held my breath now, my gaze fixed upon one portion of the heavens, hoping I might see a shooting star.

Instead, I saw Flora, falling from above as she had earlier in the day, her plane trailing blue smoke, her red parachute opening from her chest as if her heart itself were unfurling. I saw Ben and my mother again, and realized that neither of them had spoken a word all afternoon. I wanted to tell them what I was imagining, so that I might release them from their silence and their sadness. I imagined telling them of how, watching Flora, I had imagined I could unbutton my chest and let my own heart billow out and lift me to the skies, from where I would look down upon all the sleeping men, women, and children of the world. And as I floated over villages and cities, I would choose stories from those I had been saving, and then I would descend, and give them away, one by one— house by house and room by room—inserting them into people's dreams.

I heard a scraping sound, metal on metal, like the sound the propeller made when Izzie had cranked it before climbing into his bi-plane.

I pictured the moment again: all of us standing on the open plains of the Palisades where, a few years before, when Karl had been with us, we made most of our cowboy movies. Flora's plane was already high in the sky above.

Izzie's plane rolled toward the cliff's edge, turned, and came toward us, then lifted off from the ground, above our heads, heading for the island of Manhattan before circling back. The ratcheting sound of the engine, like that of a hundred machine guns, was deafening.

The metal scraping ceased and in the sky above I saw Izzie, who, having walked from the wing of his plane onto the wing of Flora's, had cut the engine of Flora's plane. The plane glided soundlessly. Flora, in the uniform of a German aviator, stood on the wing where Izzie had been, and she leapt out into space.

The plane dipped, then swirled downward in a careening spiral. Mister Bitzer followed it with his camera while

Mister Griffith shouted at him not to stop—that there would still be time to film Flora, floating in her parachute above, after Izzie's plane had reached the river.

But when Izzie's plane was less than fifty yards from the water's surface, at the point where he always stopped his falling leaf and rose into the air, the engine cranked, but did not catch.

My heart stopped, and I grabbed for my mother's hand.

An instant later, Izzie's plane exploded against the river.

Magnificent! Mister Griffith said. And now, Billy, my man—the evil Hun!

Mister Bitzer tilted his camera upwards, aimed it at Flora.

I kept my eyes on the water's surface, and I imagined Izzie standing at the bottom of the river, his aviator's cap buttoned tight under his chin, his boots stuck fast in sludge. In his hands he held a wedding bouquet of yellow tea roses.

Miss Gish moved swiftly to the edge of the cliff and removed her coat. Would she dive in to rescue him? Her body was nearly as slight as my own, so that I was frightened the wind might push her over the edge. She saw me approach, and pointed to the water below.

There! she exclaimed, taking my hand in hers. Look—!

Through chunks of floating metal and wood, Izzie's head appeared. He waved to us, and started swimming through the smoke and flames.

Hey Griff, he said, several minutes later, you know what you should do?

What? Mister Griffith asked.

You should go fly a kike.

Izzie and Flora wiped grease from each other's bodies with large green towels.

I heard voices. I stood and pressed my back against the trunk of the chestnut tree. The metal scraping, I realized, was that of the cemetery gate being unlocked.

She spoke. I took the key from Father Balsamo, that's where I got it. Where'd you think?

You're nuts, he said. You really are.

No, she said. *Your* nuts.

Hey, take it easy on a guy.

You listen, hey—I found the key to the graveyard, so what you gotta find is the key to my heart, yeah?

Her voice was harsh, her accent strong like that of most of the Italians who lived in the row houses near the Atlantic Highlands and worked in the radiator factory there.

Only first you gotta find me, she said. Hide and seek, and you're it. Start counting—

Wait a second—where are you? Where the hell are you?

I'm hiding.

I told you before. I ain't in the mood for your crazy games no more.

Oh yeah? Then go on home. Go tell Father Balsamo on me. Only watch out, 'cause I already told him on you.

You *what*?

While I was snitching the key I made up these stories to get him all hot, about the wild things you and me been doing together.

You bitch. You goddamn bitch. If I catch you, I'll beat the shit out of you.

Aw—I bet you say that to all the girls.

Where the hell are you?

I told you—I'm hiding.

If I find you I'm gonna screw your no-good dago brains out.

Is that a promise?

Yeah.

Then I'm hiding under the big chestnut tree.

Hi, I said.

Hey there, what's up? she replied, and she said it in a way that made me think she had *expected* to find me waiting for her.

Backlit by the moon, everything about her was dark— her neck, her lips, her hair, her eyes.

You're Little Joey, ain't you?

Yes.

You're the kid who used to play all them weird girls' parts in moving pictures, right?

Yes.

Her black hair swirled wildly around her face, and I closed my eyes, slipped inside one of her curls as if into a whirlpool, and rode on it, down and around, around and down.

I didn't mean nothing bad, about you being weird, she said. Weird's a good word with me.

Me too.

She laughed. It figures, the parts you played, she said.

Ready or not, here I come—

What luck, she said. I mean, I was thinking all day— yeah, I'll meet Vito in the cemetery—sure—but that ain't what's gonna be important, because today's my lucky day—I just woke up knowing, with the full moon and all—that something *different* was gonna happen for me today.

I thought of telling her about the scene I'd performed for Ben, as the young bride, and of how, after that, I had worked for the rest of the day with Mister Griffith.

Okay, she said. This is what we'll do. I'll give him what he wants and get rid of him, yeah? Then we can get acquainted, you and me.

Yes.

You're not scared?

No.

Yes you are. Your palm's wet. But don't be scared. I'll be back before you can say Jack Robinson.

Jack Robinson.

You said it. She laughed, backed away, cocked her head to one side. So tell me the truth now, she said. Wouldn't I look *terrific* in moving pictures?

Who the hell you talking to?

She moved away, and when he saw her and grabbed her around the waist, she grabbed at his hair, pulling his face to hers. They kissed for a long time, then moved off, up and over the northern slope of the cemetery, then down again, circling back, until their heads were level with the heads of the gravestones nearer to me.

They disappeared from view, and once again, though I could not see them, I could hear them.

Don't play me for no sap, he said. That's all I ask.

I never play you for a sap, Vito, she said. Trust me, please? *Please*—?

I asked you once already—who the hell were you talking to?

The moon, that's who.

I heard a cracking sound, bone against flesh.

There's more where that came from, you ever cheat on me.

Up yours.

No. Up yours, sister.

I heard her cry out. Oh Jesus, not there—easy! Easy does it, Vito. Christ! Easy. Wait. Please wait—

You love me?

Please, goddamnit. Please. Just wait till I—oh Jesus, something's gonna bust for sure, and it ain't gonna be my heart.

Tell me you love me. C'mon—

Please, Vito, I'm begging you. Please just take it easy and we'll both live longer.

But you like it, right? You like doing it here, with all the damned corpses. That's why you stole the key.

No. It's not that way. I just thought it would be quiet and romantic here.

It's spooky is what it is.

Please stop. I don't *like* it when you hurt me.

Then tell me. C'mon. You never tell me enough. Tell me.

I love you, she said.

Again!

I love you.

Say it different. Use all those words the way you know how. Talk to me.

I never loved nobody like I love you, Vito, she said. I love you like I love my own heart. I never dreamt I could love nobody the way I love you. I love you more than life itself. I can't live without you. Anything you want I'll give you because without you I'd die, that's how much I love you. . . .

Her voice faded, then disappeared. I watched bats fly out across the sky, then dip down between trees, like fighter planes.

Gentle, my love, I heard her say a few moments later. Gentle. Please. Oh please, my darling. Oh gentle, gentle.

I imagined that her dark eyes, reflecting fire from the moon, were ovals of silver, and that the silver was melting along her cheeks.

All she ever wanted, she said, was for him to be gentle with her and she would do anything he wanted. Was that too much to ask?

He didn't answer, but I imagined that he was inside her, from behind, as if he were the back part of a centaur and she the torso and head. I saw her staring upwards, her eyes closed, the moon's rays piercing her eyelids, journeying downward to her heart.

I saw Bobby Harron kissing the Negro soldier and I thought of how pictures, like love, could move through your eyes and down to your heart without ever passing through words.

With my back pressed against the iron rails of the fence, I held one chestnut in my right hand and three in my left.

I did not remember having moved out from under the tree, up the slope, between the gravestones, and down again to the cemetery fence, but I was there, beside the gate, and I could see the two of them clearly now.

I saw her swing at him, but he caught her wrist, bent her arm backwards.

Give?

Never.

He bent her arm further back so that I was frightened it would snap in two. She laughed.

C'mon, Gloria. Don't make me do it. Give up, bitch. Give—do you give?

He wrenched her arm hard, and she fell to the ground.

I warned you never to laugh at me, he said. You know I get nuts when people laugh at me.

I realized that I was starting to see the three of us as if on strips of film Ben and I had cut up and hung on wooden racks to dry, so I stopped, because I knew that if I made what was happening into pictures, or into a story, I would be unable to act.

She laughed again, and when he pulled her up by the hair, I was ready: I stood, took a deep breath, and threw.

The chestnut cracked against his cheekbone.

Hey!

He turned toward me and I threw again, sidearm this time. I missed and he rushed at me, enraged. I waited until he was no more than ten yards away and then I threw again, hitting him square in the middle of his face.

Blood spurted at once and he grabbed for his nose, as if he were a clown pulling at a balloon.

Who the hell—?

He pulled at his trousers, which had fallen to his ankles. Across the moonlit leaves, an enormous shadow flowed toward me. On the other side of the cemetery fence, a black owl the size of a bear seemed to hover in the air. I dropped down, close to the ground.

The owl's shadow moved across mine. Vito looked past me, let go of his trousers.

Holy shit! he cried. It's Father Balsamo.

The priest raised his arms, his cape rising with them, blocking the moon's light. Then he swooped forward, and Vito took off across the cemetery, one hand at his waist to keep his trousers from falling, his other arm moving in circles, as if he were an organ grinder.

Gloria was next to me, holding to my arm. You got some aim, kid, she said. I bet his nose is broke.

Silhouetted against the moon, Vito zigzagged in a galloping motion between gravestones and mausoleums, further and further from us—growing smaller and smaller—with Father Balsamo, like a small fat bat, in pursuit.

Vito stumbled and rose, stumbled again, cursed Gloria, cursed his father, cursed Jesus Christ.

Father Balsamo fell upon Vito, lifted him from the ground by the throat. Vito's trousers, like a harlequin's collar, lay bunched around his ankles. Gloria laughed, leaned against my shoulder for balance and then, suddenly, her body stiffened.

No! she said. Oh no. . . .

From the sleeve of his cassock, Father Balsamo withdrew what appeared to be a whip.

Gloria pressed my head to her bosom. Don't look, she said.

Her perfume, like lilacs in spring, but with another fragrance, stronger yet sweeter still, as if from the damp earth in which lilacs grew, made me dizzy.

Shit, she said. Oh sweet Jesus, Mary, and Joseph, I didn't mean for this to happen. I really didn't. Poor Vito. Poor, sweet Vito.

With her head upon my lap, we watched the bats move above us, flying in pairs, wingtip to wingtip, as if holding hands.

If my mother woke before morning and found me missing, I knew, she would wake my father. If she woke my father, he would fetch Izzie and they would set out to search for me.

And when Father Balsamo and Vito's father were finished with him, Vito would come hunting for Gloria. But the meaner Father Balsamo and Vito's father were to him, Gloria believed, the sooner he would want to escape with her so they could start a life of their own.

She said that Vito was going to make a terrific father—that he could chew your ear off about all the great things he was going to do for the children he and Gloria would have someday.

I asked what he would do for me, if he found me with her.

He'd chop off your little fire engine, she said.

What would he do to you? I asked.

I hate to imagine, she said.

I like to imagine, I said.

She laughed. You're really cockeyed, ain't you?

I hope so.

You're the original cockeyed wonder.

That's me.

In the cool autumn air, Gloria smelled like spring—like freshly turned earth and young grass. And in the spring, were we to lie together, she would, I imagined, smell like autumn—sweet and musky, like burning leaves.

That was why I believed we would be friends forever.

But I kept myself from saying so because I was afraid that if I did, my words might frighten her away. Instead, I told her I'd come to the cemetery to collect chestnuts.

Vito, he's a real chest nut too, she laughed, and touched her breasts.

I looked away, frightened she might want me to touch her—frightened she might ask me to say more—to tell her everything I was thinking and feeling. Yet if I kept anything from her, I knew, that would mean I did not trust her in the way I believed you had to trust someone you loved. I didn't know what to do, but I knew that the mixture of peace and danger—of lying quietly with a woman whose presence could cause me harm—excited me.

I said that one day I would make a moving picture just for her, and that it would be the best moving picture anyone would ever make.

Promises—always promises, she said. Especially since everyone knows you and your family stopped making pictures a couple years back.

I said that we hadn't stopped making them—we'd just stopped showing them.

Because of what happened to your mother?

Yes, I said, but also because my Uncle Ben says it's easier to make the moving pictures we want if we don't think about what's going to happen to them afterwards.

But if we didn't sell our movies, Gloria wanted to know, what did we live on?

I told her about my Uncle Karl sending us money for work we did for him—developing and cutting film, putting in titles—and for jobs we did for people Karl worked with, the way we'd done for Mister Griffith today.

But even when we don't do work for him, he sends us money, I said. He doesn't use his own money to make pictures anymore. That's the first secret, he says. Always to use other people's money.

Nice work if you can get it, Gloria said.

He works mostly with Mister Zukor and Mister Laemmle, I said, but also with Mister Loew and Mister Fox, and sometimes with Mister Schenck.

Schenck! Gloria exclaimed. What a guy. I worked for him when he and his brother first opened Palisades Park. He was this really tall man with a big Russian accent and he used to try to cop a feel whenever he could. That was before he married what's-her-name—

Norma Talmadge.

Yeah. That's the one. She was some looker, her and her sisters too. At the Park, I sold tickets for rides, see, and I'll say this, that even though I wouldn't put out for him, he always treated me fair. So listen, I'll make you a deal: you can make a moving picture for me, like you said—even make one *about* me if you want—only not the way your uncle says. You have to promise to be sure people see it afterwards.

Why?

So I can be somebody.

But you *are* somebody.

You don't understand. Listen for a minute, okay? I thought about it a lot, almost every time I been in a moving picture theater—or even when I go to one of them run-down

Mutoscope parlors we still got near where I live. This is what I thought: I live the life I live and if I'm here or I'm gone, who gives a crap? But if once, just once, you put my face and story up there on a screen for millions of people to see, then I'll matter to people forever after.

But why would you want to matter to millions of people you don't know?

Just stay shut and listen, yeah? Jesus, you're some stubborn kid.

Probably, I said.

So listen to what I say, then. I want to be a somebody—not a nobody my whole life, okay? When people see me on the street, I want them to stop and wish they were me. I want men to be begging for me just to look at them—and then when I'm rich and famous, I want Vito to eat his heart out for missing his chance.

You want lots of things, I said.

You bet your sweet life I do. So you promise to make a movie about me that gets into all the theaters, and I promise to be your friend for always, okay?

Okay.

It's a deal?

It's a deal.

I put out my hand for her to shake, and she took my hand but then, with amazing quickness, she moved above me and kissed me on the mouth.

The shock of her lips on mine was wonderful.

So tell me what other secrets your uncle give you, she said.

She was lying down again, her head on my lap. I stared at her mouth, upside down, and wished it were mine. My own lips were burning and I had to suck in large amounts of air to catch my breath.

Just business stuff, I said. He says his brother Ben is a genius at making pictures, but where does it get him? He says the secret's not in making moving pictures, but in controlling distribution, so that the thing to do is to be like Mister Edison—not to put your energy and brains into pictures, but into patents and sales—but that Mister Edison missed his big chance when he didn't patent moving pictures, because he thought they were just something to go along with the phonograph.

Okay, she said, and she turned over, rested her chin in her palms. I got a secret for you. Are you ready?

Yes.

I like the way you *look*. I always wanted to be able to get close to you like this, so I could tell you.

I feel the same.

You like the way you look?

No, I said, and she laughed.

The truth is, she said, I always wished I could have a kid brother like you. A friend I could talk to without worrying about the other stuff that always happens with guys, when all they're really after is to get under your skirt. That's why I believe it's such great good luck we found each other tonight.

But it wasn't luck, I said. It's what happened—it's what really was.

Maybe, Gloria said. But the truth is, I'll be your friend anyway, even if you never make the movie, so don't worry about promises coming true or not. But you still owe me one.

One what?

One secret. Only make it from yourself this time, not from one of your uncles.

I took a deep breath and then I told her about my mother saying nearly every day of my life that I should have been born a girl, and my father echoing her most of the time, but—and this was the *real* secret, I said quickly—that even though other people, like Ben, thought this was a terrible thing for them to do to me, I never really minded.

I like feeling like a girl, I said. Sometimes I think that if I could have one wish come true in life it would be to be a beautiful woman like you.

I know what you mean, Gloria said. Because when I was

a little girl I used to think I was twins, see, but I used to make up that my other half was living inside me, right here—she placed my hand against her stomach—except tucked up under my rib cage.

Maybe, she said, if you decided you had another person hiding inside you the way we did—a girl inside me and a boy inside you—it could be like having a child of your own growing up inside you who you could take care of and raise up in ways you yourself were never raised.

She was silent for a while, and then she spoke again: I was eighteen years old last month, so I'm legal, see. Whatever we do from now on, me and Vito, especially when we have our kids, the responsibility's on our heads.

She asked me how old I was, and I told her I was fourteen, but that I'd be fifteen soon.

It wasn't so crazy to think the way she did, she said, because where she worked, in the laundry at St. Mary's Hospital, the nurses told her about children who were born with dead children—or parts of children—living inside them, near their hearts. They saw them when young women gave birth or when doctors had to open up them up if they died of the flu epidemic, to examine their lungs. The nurses said they looked like the babies you saw floating in jars at Coney Island.

With my fingers, I started outlining the sockets of Gloria's eyes. When my mother's eyes got red and swollen from all the lights, I said, I'd rub them like this.

She was some looker, your mother. You look like her, you know. It's what makes you so beautiful for a guy.

I hope so.

I mean, it's really lousy, what happened to her.

I used to put drops of castor oil in her eyes too, I said, and sometimes when they hurt really bad—if we had to be under hot lights all day—I'd make compresses by wrapping slices of raw potato between strips of damp gauze and laying them across her eyes.

Gloria closed her eyes.

By the time we woke up, the moon had traveled across the heavens into the western sky, and it came at us sideways, from low on the horizon, glancing over dead leaves as if skimming across a dark lake.

Would you tell me the story again, Gloria asked, of how your family's business got its name?

So I told her the story the way Ben had told it to me when I was a child.

Once upon a time the Wind challenged the Sun to see who was more powerful, and the Wind pointed down to Earth, to where an old man, with a cane, was walking. Why, I wager I can make that man take his coat off before you can, the Wind boasted.

The Sun remained silent, and the Wind drew air into its cheeks and blew with all its might upon the old man. When the old man felt the force of the Wind, he let go of his cane and pulled his coat tight around him.

The Wind puffed out its cheeks once more, and let loose with an enormous blast of frigid air. The man drew his coat closer. Enraged, the Wind blew harder, and continued, all through the night, to howl and rage and vent its breath upon the man.

When morning came, the Sun rose in the East, as it did each day, and it found the old man fast asleep by the side of the road, his ragged coat rolled tight around him. Soon the old man sat up and rose to his feet. He stretched, and, feeling the warmth of the Sun upon him, he smiled and took off his coat.

Gloria was staring at me so hard I thought her eyes would burn holes in me.

God, but you got a gorgeous mouth, she said. She took out a lipstick from the pocket of her dress.

Would you let me make you up now, like you promised?

Yes.

I been wanting to ever since I first saw you. You got some beautiful mouth for a boy your size.

She drew lipstick on my mouth, the wax like warm satin

from having been close to her body, and in return for the story I'd told, she said, she would recite a poem she'd been saving for Vito but hadn't had the chance to give to him.

While she recited the poem, I transformed the words into letters I would use to make the poem into a title—into what the bride would think moments before she learns that her beloved has perished:

> WITH MY HEAD UPON YOUR HEART
> HOLD ME CLOSE AND NEVER WAKE ME—
> SING ME DEAD AND KISS ME DEAD—
> HEART AND SOUL AND BODY—TAKE ME. . . .

Most of the time, Vito loves when I recite poems to him, she said. I bet that surprises you, don't it?

Yes.

He's a lot sweeter than he looks. He keeps count of the number of times I tell him I love him, and if it's less one week than it was the week before, he gets mad.

I said nothing.

Hey—are you angry with me?

No.

With Vito, right?

I guess.

If you knew him like I do, you'd feel different. We got that in common, me and Vito—being scared the people we want to have love us are gonna hurt us—from how we both got knocked around so much when we were kids.

But he should stop.

Sure. And the moon should be made out of cheese.

I blotted my lips on a tissue. Gloria outlined my eyes with a pencil, placed a black dot at the inside corner of each of my eyes, and worked on my lashes with a tiny black brush.

There, she said. You can open your eyes now.

She drew a mirror from her pocket and held it up so I could see how I looked.

Thank you, I said.

Thank you? she said back. That's all you got to say?

You did a good job.

Good!? I did a *terrific* job!

The woman in the mirror was a woman I had never seen before, but I didn't say so to Gloria. Instead, I looked through the mirror until the image dissolved, so that where my face had been, the story for Gloria's moving picture began to appear.

This is what I saw: A poor young woman gazing into a mirror sees a man gazing back at her. The man looks at her with such steadiness that her heart quickens and she turns away, for she cannot believe a woman in her lowly position could ever in this life be loved by such a man.

While I watched the woman leave her flat and walk through the city, I explained to Gloria that we called our studio the Sun and Wind Company because if we had done it the other way around, Wind and Sun, people might have thought it was the name of a father and son company. I told her my mother used to say the name was perfect since Ben was like the Sun, hardly ever saying anything, and Karl was like the Wind, always talking too much.

But while I talked I kept watching the woman in Gloria's story. I watched her walk through the city toward the waterfront, where, on the wharf, sailors cast lewd glances her way and hurled insults at her. In her black coat and shawl, photographed against the blackness of the water, it was almost as if she were not there. She looked down into the water, and imagined the comfort she might find within it—for drowning, she believes, like love, can bring peace and an end to pain.

Then, on the surface of the water, I saw the reflection of a man's face.

Hey, Gloria said, passing her hand in front of my eyes. Are you okay?

Are you all right, my child? I heard the man ask.

I said I'd never felt better and, my eyes open, I watched

the man order the Jackies who were insulting the woman to move along.

We better get going then, Gloria said. I'm gonna catch hell as is—and we gotta get you back before any cops come after us.

The man, I now saw, dressed in a hat and topcoat, was the man whose face the woman had seen in her mirror.

I watched the man escort her through the city. I watched him feed her, clothe her, nurse her back to health, and I saw the woman, grateful and adoring, give herself to him.

Gloria unlocked the gate.

Sometimes, she said, Vito swears he'll kill himself if I ever left him, that's how much he loves me.

He didn't act it, I said.

You're jealous, she said.

No I'm not.

Not much, Gloria said. *Guys*! You don't give a crap about us, whether we live or die, but if you think for a second we got our hand on some other fella's business, you go nuts.

He hurt you, I said.

Yeah. Well I hurt him too, in my time. I hurt him where he lives.

Where does he live?

Where he lives—it's an expression. It means I know how to get to him—to make him jealous so I can get what I want when I want it. Listen: I'm a lot smarter than I look.

I saw the man enter another house, and I saw that in this house he had a wife and three young children. I saw the woman whose life he saved discover a photo of his family in the pocket of his jacket. I saw her show him the photo, and I watched him laugh at her. Had he ever denied he was married? Had he ever promised her anything?

Gloria stopped. Hey—are you all right? she asked. I got a jar of cold cream with me, to wipe off the makeup before you get home if you're worried about that. Only how are we gonna snap you out of these trances you keep going into?

I don't know, I said, even while I was imagining the bar-

barous things the man might ask of the woman, and that she might agree to, in order to keep his love—all those things I would have to invent, and then enact, scene by scene, in front of a camera.

I saw the woman's face as she begged for his love and his mercy. But why, I wondered, was I imagining a man so mean-spirited—a man who thrived on making women slaves to love—when I was feeling so happy to be with Gloria?

Do you and Vito really want to have a child?

She patted her stomach, took my hand, placed it there. We got one in the oven already, she said.

Really? I said. And then: I mean—does he know?

Not yet.

I felt faint suddenly. I leaned upon the gate for balance and closed my eyes. The first time you saw the woman, she was holding a newborn child in her arms. I saw her in an iris shot, and then, as the iris opened, I saw that the child was not hers, but belonged to a mother who lay in a hospital bed, and into whose loving arms the woman placed the infant.

I saw the moving picture's final scene: the woman lying in the hospital bed where the mother and infant had previously lain. A priest was there now, however, along with the Sisters of Mercy, and they surrounded the bed where the childless young woman was being given the Sacrament of Extreme Unction.

Yet you would not, were the pictures reversed, be able to tell the difference—between the opening and closing shots—between the woman's face when gazing with joy at the newborn child and the woman's face when gazing, near death, at eternity.

So ain't you gonna say something to me? Gloria asked.

I'm very happy for you, I said. Only I'm scared too.

Yeah, she said softly. Me too.

She took my hand, and we walked back toward town.

For some of our moving pictures, when we needed a baby for a part, I explained, we would rent one from a Negro orphanage. Karl used to pick them out and bring them across from New York City on the ferry because on screen their eyes came out darker and more mysterious than the eyes of white babies.

No wonder they always look so gorgeous, Gloria said. Nigger babies—go figure.

Your eyes are like that.

Yeah, that's me. My mother thought I was a freak when I was born, because she couldn't see the pupils in my eyes.

By the time I get home, everyone will be awake, I said.

You're the only one who knows about me and my baby, she said. Does that scare you?

No. But I'm scared of what might happen to you when you go home and Vito's waiting.

Ah, if he lays even a finger on me, my brothers'll beat the crap out of him. And I got this too, she said, touching her stomach again. I can threaten to tell on him. Only you tell me this, Joey—if your mother and father are waiting up for you, what are *you* gonna do?

Make up a story.

About what?

I don't know, I said.

Why not?

Because I didn't make it up yet.

She laughed, and then, for the rest of the way home, we talked about moving pictures—about our favorite actors and actresses and our favorite scenes, and we agreed that talking about moving pictures was probably the best way for people to find out if they liked each other. For there was no surer way to feel your heart rise than to say to a friend that you thought a certain movie was terrific and to have the friend say back to you that he thought it was terrific too.

And there was no quicker way to feel your heart sink than to have the opposite happen: to say that you loved a movie, or an actor, or actress, or scene, and to have the other person disagree with you.

Gloria's favorite scene of all time, she said, was from *The Cheat*, when Fannie Ward is in court for killing the man who kept her, and they ask her why she did it. I shot Arakan and this is my defense! she proclaims, and then she pulls down the shoulder of her dress to show where her lover had used a branding iron on her.

I never get that picture out of my head, Gloria said, of him putting the red-hot iron to her flesh and burning it into her.

We were nearly home, walking along the trolley tracks that curved around onto my street, and I was explaining to Gloria how we did my double roles—how you kept part of the set covered with black cloth so you didn't expose that part of the film when you photographed it, and how you back-cranked, uncovered the dark half and covered up the part of the scene you'd already shot, put on new makeup and costumes, and then cranked the film forward again—when Gloria stopped.

I think I better make myself scarce, she said, and she pointed to a spot on the roof of our building, above the letters that spelled out the words PICTURE COMPANY. My mother was sitting there, eating her breakfast under a red-and-white beach umbrella, while, a few feet away, on top of a telephone pole we had lashed like a ship's mast to a corner of the roof, Izzie was standing straight up in the air, but upside down on his head.

Izzie was reading his morning newspaper, the way he liked to at the start of each day.

He does that a lot, I said. It's how he practices his balance. Sometimes he gets me and my father to wiggle the pole but he never falls off.

My father leaned over the edge of the roof, called down to me to hurry and come upstairs, to take the elevator. He was wearing a white handkerchief across his nose and mouth, so that he looked like a bank robber. Izzie stayed where he was, turning the pages of his newspaper, one page at a time.

What Vito used to do—his secret, Gloria said—was after he stored his chestnuts in a cigar box for a few weeks and drilled holes in them, he painted them with clear nail polish.

Yes.

So you be good now, Joey, yeah? You be careful. You be a killer, with the chestnuts *and* the ladies, you hear, and you don't take crap from nobody. Keep your pants on and your nose clean.

Then she kissed me on the mouth, after which she was gone, heading back in the direction from which we'd come.

When our elevator let me out onto the roof, my father told me that Izzie refused to come down from the telephone pole because he wanted to keep the blood in his body flowing toward his head.

He has the plague, my mother said.

It's true, my father said. His back aches and he has a fever. He was coughing up black phlegm all night long.

Quinine, Epsom salt, and mustard plasters, my mother said. I told him what to do: quinine, Epsom salt, and mustard plasters. Your health comes first, I explained. You can always kill yourself later. But talking to Izzie is like talking to the wall. Like Poppa used to say, a fool can throw a stone into the water that ten wise men can't recover. Sure. But do I care? Am I the fool? Look at him up there with black blood running out of his nose. You look at him, and then tell me who the fool is.

Here, Ben said, and without asking, he tied a handkerchief around my nose and mouth to keep the influenza germs away. Don't mind your mother, he whispered. She'll be all right now that you're home.

Don't spit, my mother said. You can get arrested for spitting, or for sneezing, if you don't sneeze into a handkerchief. I want you to be careful, Joey. Lick a stamp and lick the Kaiser is what I say. Asking Izzie to take care of himself is like asking a Jew the way out of Poland.

She's been like this all day, Ben said. Ever since Izzie climbed up the pole and she called for you and you didn't come.

First goes my nose and then my toes, my mother said. And then we said farewell to us making pictures together. So why shouldn't Karl leave for California? And why shouldn't Ben hide downstairs all the time with my son, doing who-knows-what. The way I look at it, gentlemen, is that now it's Izzie's turn to go away forever and forsake me.

Well, I look on the positive side, my father said. Izzie never takes chances. If he could survive crashing into the river, he can certainly survive influenza.

The epidemic doesn't live in the river, my mother said. It's too smart.

Izzie waved the newspaper and called down to us. They closed all the theaters in New York City, it says here, he said. But they're letting the schools stay open. Last week they cancelled the fight between Dempsey and Levinsky, and get this—this week they're banning *all* boxing matches.

But they found a new cure, my father said. I read about it yesterday. What they do, is they take serum from people who got well and give it to those who are ill.

They can take my blood any time they want, my mother said. After all, they've taken everything else—except for my husband, my son, and my breakfast. But perhaps if Izzie comes down and does what I told him, everything will be all right.

Izzie! I called. *Izzie*!

Hey, how's my favorite guy? Izzie answered.

Please come down, I said. I have something to show you.

I held up my cloth sack, so he could see my chestnuts.

Flora stood next to me, wearing her German aviator's hat, her face hidden behind a veil of white gauze.

"Somebody loves me," my mother sang. "I wonder who. I wonder who he can be . . . " Simon, fetch me more tea, and a sweet roll.

Come on down, you big jerk, Flora called.

I'm looking for good news, Izzie shouted. As soon as I find good news, I'll be there.

Listen to what I'm telling you, Joey, my mother said to me. Everybody leaves you in the end. That's the main thing to remember. Didn't I always say so? So who can a boy trust in this world? Come here and kiss your mother good morning and tell her a story.

I went to my mother, who did not move, but continued to stare out across the rooftops, to the river. I bent my head down, below the wide white brim of her summer hat. Pressing my lips to her veil, and her veil to her cheek, I kissed her.

You smell like lilacs, she said.

I call it a miracle, my father said. That without a nose, she can still smell.

Don't talk like a jackass, Simon, my mother said. Go and fetch the tea.

I saw leaves floating on a lake, the woman slipping down through the leaves. I watched her mouth turn from black to gray when the man begins to beat her, so that you would think you could reach out and peel her lips from the screen.

Where did the perfume come from? my mother asked, and before I could reply she spoke again. As if I didn't know, she said. As if I didn't know that sooner or later you'd find somebody else.

Izzie sneezed, blood spraying from his nose.

It is now estimated that more people have died from the influenza pandemic than died in the war, Izzie said. It says so right here.

It's always the same, my mother said, standing and walking to the elevator. In the large open space behind the elevator Ben and I planned to build a rotating stage like Mister Edison's, that, driven by motors, would keep turning in the direction of the sun, to make use of natural light all day long. My mother slid open the gate to the elevator's cage, shifted the handle on the control panel, and sent the elevator back to the ground floor.

Women want to be beautiful and men want to be wealthy, she said. That's all you need to know. So what else is new? Fetch me my tea, Simon, but take away the dirty dishes first.

My father put cups and dishes, along with the teapot,

onto a tray. He winked at me and walked to the elevator. My mother stepped out of the way.

The elevator was not there. Stop! I called out. Father—please! *Stop*—!

Shush, my mother said to me. Don't be ridiculous, Joey. Let your father do what he wants.

Ah, here's some good news at last, Izzie called down. Ninety percent of all moving picture studios in California have been shut down for four weeks.

My father grinned and, holding the tray out in front of him and telling my mother he would be right back with a fresh pot of tea and a warm sweet roll—looking backwards over his shoulder, winking at me again, and unable to see through the tray to the floor below—he stepped out into the empty elevator shaft.

Flora laughed, said that my father walked exactly the way Buster Keaton did.

He's as thin and as dumb, my mother said. But he didn't get to marry one of the Talmadge girls. He got me instead.

My mother spoke to Ben: You should get this on film, she said.

In truth, my father's step, before he stopped walking on air and plummeted downwards in the elevator shaft, was quite graceful.

He never let go of the tray.

Oh my God, Ben said, and he ran to the staircase and hurried to the floor below.

Izzie's newspaper fluttered in the air while Izzie, like a monkey, clambered down his telephone pole.

My mother walked back to her chair. She sat under the beach umbrella and looked out toward the harbor at ferries, tug boats, and tankers.

I grasped the elevator gate and looked down at my father, who lay on top of the cage as if he were fast sleep.

I imagined Gloria, in a nurse's uniform, tending to Izzie, peeling a mustard plaster from his chest, the plaster leaving a large triangular mark, like a brand, on his skin.

Without thinking, I leapt down toward the roof of the elevator cage, screaming all the way, and realizing that, an instant before, during his fall, no least sound had risen from my father's mouth.

1921

My father entered the room, not from the door I would use when we filmed the scene a second time—a scene in which Mister Gardner and Laura would kiss for the first time—but from the open side of the platform. His face bright with curiosity, he approached a large sheet of glass that was fixed in an upright position beside the divan and, eyes closed, he ran his palm across the glass's upper edge, tracing its silhouette.

I know, he said, opening his eyes. It's a woman, isn't it?

Yes, I said.

But where did she come from?

You made her.

But how?

I explained that he had used a pantograph to transfer the woman's outline from a strip of film onto a large sheet of paper. Then he had cut out the shape and taped the paper to glass, after which, using a glazier's knife, he had carved the woman's figure.

Amazing, he said. He touched the glass gently with his fingertips. Well, he remarked, it's certainly easy to see through *this* woman, isn't it?

Same old Simon, Karl said. He may have lost his mind, but he's still got his sense of humor.

My father turned to me. And who are you? he asked.

I'm your son.

Amazing, he said. But I'll tell you this, young man. You look more like a famous moving picture actor to me than a son. In fact, you resemble Bobby Harron quite a bit. I knew Bobby Harron. I saw him fight in the war. I saw him fall in love with Miss Gish, and I saw him try to save the life of his courageous colored comrade.

Bobby Harron's dead, my mother said. He died last year.

Dead? my father said, tears appearing in his eyes at once. Poor Bobby. I remember when he was just a messenger boy working for Mister Griffith. But he rescued Miss Gish when she was floating on the ice, you know.

No, I said. That was Mister Barthelmess.

My father looked puzzled. You're probably right, he said. My memory isn't what it used to be, alas. I've been working under a handicap ever since, so they tell me, I fell down an elevator shaft.

I considered telling my father the truth: that Bobby Harron had killed himself in a New York City hotel room on the night *Way Down East* opened. Many people believed he had journeyed east from California in order to commit the act because Mister Griffith had excluded him from a film with Miss Gish, just as Miss Gish, with whom Bobby was madly in love, had excluded him from her life.

But I said nothing. All I cared about was having Gloria by my side, telling me it was time to leave. I imagined that Gloria's children, Angelina and Marco, were with us, eager to set out on our journey west.

My father touched my cheek with the back of his hand. Your skin is wonderfully smooth, he said. Like Bobby Harron's. Can you remember how beautiful Miss Gish looked while she drifted toward the waterfall? Can you remember when the horse tumbled into the water beside her and The

Gentle Stranger brought her to shore and asked her to marry him?

So now you see for yourself, my mother said to Karl, why with Simon, what I say is this: that the elevator just doesn't go to the top of the shaft anymore.

Stop, Ben said. For God's sake, Hannah. Please—

My mother laughed. Why? He's still my husband, she said. And believe me when I tell you I'd love to be happy the way he is. It would be a dream come true to be able to forget so much.

It's true, my father said. I'm a very happy man.

My mother rested her head on his shoulder. Do you love me, Simon? she asked.

Oh yes, my father said. I love you. But tell me again, please—who are you?

I'm your wife.

Ah yes, Simon said. And I certainly love my wife. And let me tell you what else I love. I love bridges and tunnels, especially when they're filled with trains. And I adore trains— steam, diesel, or electric. He turned to me. Have you ever traveled to the great city across the river, young man, and watched them cut open the ground in order to build the new subway lines? Would you like to visit me in my room and see the models of bridges and tunnels I've constructed there?

Yes, I said. Only I've already been there with you.

Then tell me this: what year is it now?

It's 1921.

Ah, then they've already *finished* building the IRT line, as well as the Hell's Gate Bridge, the tunnels below the East River, and the tubes to New Jersey. Many men have died in the enterprise, you know. Some have been buried alive. Still, someday soon, mark my word, they're going to build a bridge from here to New York City, clear across the Hudson River.

See how happy he is, my mother said to Karl. Sometimes, in this life, my brother, you get lucky.

So stay lucky, Hannah, and come with me to California, Karl urged, as he had been doing ever since his arrival that morning. Please, Hannah—Ben—Joey. Listen to me for once in your lives. When I didn't have the money, I didn't have it, but now I have it, and I want us to be together again—a family!—the way we were in the old days, but with the means to make wonderful new lives for ourselves.

Look! my father said, and he pointed to the far end of the building.

There, backlit by the morning sun, a man stood in the entranceway. When I was a child, trolleys had come through that entranceway, their electrical poles reaching two stories high to the overhead tracks from which they had secured their electricity, and from which we now hung our muslin light diffusers and our banks of klieg lights and mercury vapor lamps. As a boy, I had set pennies on the trolley tracks so I could watch sparks fly up when the trolleys passed over them.

He's here, my mother said, adjusting her veil. It's time, Simon.

My father removed a handkerchief from the breast pocket of his jacket, folded it carefully, set it upon his shoulder, then set his violin upon the handkerchief.

The man moved into the shadows. I closed my eyes and what I saw in the darkness were two figures holding hands and walking the other way—emerging *from* a tunnel—and I knew at once that what I was seeing was the first picture for the story I wanted to make in memory of Izzie.

The story would take place in a city where everyone, except for this young man and young woman, had died—a city where all the inhabitants, like Izzie, had been victims of the influenza epidemic.

My father was playing "Love's Old Sweet Song," and my mother, a hand upon his shoulder, was singing: 'Just a song at twilight . . . when the lights are low. . . .'

The man walked toward us carrying a bouquet of flowers. In the high vertical rectangle of light behind him he appeared very small, yet as he neared us I saw that he was very large. His knuckles were enormous.

I am Carlo Vallone, he said. He took off his hat, bowed to my mother, and presented her with the bouquet. Carlo Vallone was one of the men for whom Vito worked, transporting boatloads of illegal alcohol across the river to New York City and Brooklyn, and down the coast to Cape May, Atlantic City, and Red Bank.

Quick, Karl whispered to Ben. Camera! . . . Camera!

Ben removed a camera from his tripod, fixed a different camera in its place, gauged the light, rotated several lenses, stepped one down several stops, and began cranking. He had chosen a camera that perforated the film as it passed through the gate, punching out its own sprocket holes and producing a noise like that of a machine gun.

Carlo Vallone reached to his inside jacket pocket, withdrew a revolver. My mother laughed, pushed the gun aside, and pointed to Ben. My father had stopped playing, and was staring wide-eyed at the circles of film that came spitting out of the camera.

Confetti! he cried.

My father snatched Carlo Vallone's hat, went down on his hands and knees, and began scooping celluloid dots into the hat.

Hearing the camera's noise, I recalled the sound Izzie's plane had made on the last day he ever flew. How strange, I thought, to survive plane crashes and freezing rivers only to have your body made soft by something so tiny you could not see it. My father skipped around us in a circle, tossing confetti at my mother and Carlo Vallone.

Mayday! he cried. Mayday! He returned the empty hat to Carlo Vallone. That's French, he said. May Day comes from the French cry for help—*M'aidez! M'aidez!*

I don't speak French, and I don't want your help, Carlo Vallone said.

Please, Hannah, Karl said. Please think about coming back with me. Maybe we could even make moving pictures together again. . . .

And we could fight together again, my mother said.

Of course, Karl said, smiling. Like Poppa used to say: where there's no fight, there's no love. But then, after we enjoy a good argument, we could forgive one another. Karl put his arm around my mother, and she let her head rest on his shoulder while she listened to him talk to her about all the things he could do for us now that he was rich. He told her he was working with people in California who were planning to bring words and music to the screen. He talked about the difference between sound and silence, and how the rabbis had associated silence with slavery and words with freedom. The slave, Karl stated, lives in silence, whereas free men are always eager to tell their stories to others. That was why, he explained, the Torah has made it our duty in every generation to tell our children the story of the going forth from Egypt.

When you go religious on me, I worry, my mother said. I like you more when you talk about money.

I looked up at the overhead tracks and imagined the pungent odor and purple glow that would descend upon us later in the day when Ben and I lit our mercury vapor lamps. I imagined sitting inside a circus tent, next to the young woman who, with me, would remain alive after everyone else had died. I saw us eating cotton candy and laughing, the camera close on our faces in a moment when the last thing in the world we are capable of understanding is that the Angel of Death will soon arrive to take away every person we know and love.

My mother kissed Karl on the cheek. You'll be careful, dear brother, she said, because sometimes in his business, you see, if people are uncooperative, Carlo has them killed.

Well, with that look he has on his face, he certainly slays me, my father said.

My mother slipped her arm into Carlo Vallone's arm, gestured to my father, and led Carlo Vallone away, toward her room. My father followed, playing a wild gypsy air on his violin—walking behind them as if he were a waiter in a Hungarian restaurant.

I went around to the side of the set and checked my

makeup in a mirror. I outlined my eyes with black liner, drew crow lines from the corners of my eyes, glued on my moustache. Faint strains of violin music drifted toward me, and this meant, I knew, that in my mother's room my father was standing on one side of a Chinese screen while on the other side of the screen my mother was entertaining Carlo Vallone.

Ben set his eye to the viewfinder, signaled me with his hand, inserted the crank into its socket, and began turning it. The sound of the camera—not the racket of the perforating Mutoscope, but the more pleasant clackety-clack of our old Bell and Howell—displaced the sound of the violin.

I entered the room, pivoted, smiled my most charming smile, removed my top hat and set it down upon a gleaming mahogany table. I faced the camera, and strode directly toward the spot where I had, the day before, as Laura, been lying on the divan.

I am this man, I thought. I was that woman. I leaned down, my head passing behind the pane of glass and, in order to feel what Mister Gardner might in that moment have been feeling, I imagined being kissed by a woman who truly loved me.

I dipped my head further down, to the spot where, on the screen, Laura's lips would be awaiting mine—where, dressed as Laura, I had, the day before, been reclining—and I pressed my lips to the glass.

I always said you were the real genius in the family, Ben, Karl said. Okay. I buy it. Not the story, but the device: using the glass cutout so there won't be a line down the middle of the screen like you usually get. This is terrific. Pickford's been wanting to do *Little Lord Fauntleroy*—to play both roles the way Marie Doro doubled in *Oliver Twist*, remember?. . . and I think what you got here can do the trick. So you got a deal, brother. We're in business.

My father returned, carrying his violin.

And what kind of moving pictures do you make, sir? my father asked Ben.

We make moving pictures nobody will ever see, Ben said.

Oh they're the best kind, my father said.

Sure, Karl said. And at two bucks a seat, think of the profit, right?

My father smiled at Karl. And who are you? he asked.

I'm your brother-in-law. I produce movies.

Isn't that wonderful, my father said.

I began to peel off my moustache.

Phooey! my father exclaimed as the stench from the spirit gum escaped. Who'd ever want to kiss a man who smelled like that? No wonder you have to make love to glass women!

Then, while he held his nose closed with thumb and forefinger, he kissed me on the lips.

Ben held the film up to the light—the sequence where Laura and Mister Gardner kiss—and, with scissors, cut the strip into three discrete sections, between which sections we would insert separate close-ups of Laura and of Mister Gardner.

The kiss itself had turned out well. When I looked at the images it was difficult to recall that there were not two different people kissing. And we agreed that just before the kiss there should be a pause—a moment during which the audience would be given time to project their feelings onto my images.

With a grease pencil, Ben marked the frames he had chosen, then let me scrape the emulsion off with a razor blade, apply the glue, and place the new pieces of film—the close-ups we had shot separately on other days: of me as Laura, and of me as Mister Gardner—on top of the original film. I pressed down hard. The glue, caked under my nails, smelled bittersweet, like witch hazel mixed with honey.

Ben checked the sprocket holes to make sure they were aligned, and examined the cut under a magnifying glass. You're quite beautiful, he said. It never ceases to amaze me, Joey—how ordinary you can look most of the time, even when you're in costume and makeup and I'm photographing you, and how extraordinary you look on the film itself.

His hand on my arm, he led me to his workbench. Here, he said. Come see what I did this afternoon while you were gone.

He turned on the light beneath an old ground-glass screen. A year before, Karl had sent Ben one of the new Moviola editing machines that operated by a foot pedal like a sewing machine, and a few days earlier, in honor of Karl's visit, Ben had taken the machine from a closet and dusted it off.

Now that Karl was gone, however, Ben preferred, as ever, to do things the old way. He looked through a large magnifying glass and scanned individual frames until he came to the one he wanted.

Here, he said.

I looked through the glass, and found myself gazing down at a pair of dark eyes that gazed back up at me.

She *is* beautiful! I said.

He, Ben said, and I looked again and saw that I had been deceived by my own image: that the eyes were not, as I had assumed, Laura's, but Mister Gardner's—and that it was he and not Laura who, as Ben drew the film along under the magnifying glass, I now watched wake slowly and happily from sleep. It was morning, after their first night of love.

Is that really me? I asked, for I knew how much it pleased Ben to have me ask the question—to show him what remained, as ever, true: that I could never fully believe that the shadows we would soon project upon a screen were actually me.

Yes, it's really you, he said, and do you know what else? What?

He turned away from me and spoke again, but softly: I think this is the best moving picture we have ever made.

Yes, I exclaimed. Oh yes—!

Ben did not respond. He returned, instead, to his work, lifting strips of film from our tubs of chemicals and carrying them to the large wheels where the prints that were already fixed were drying. So that air could circulate around them more freely, the wheels stood apart at the far end of our room, next to the tiny darkroom we had boarded off and fixed up for processing our film, and the slightly larger room next to it where we did our printing. Ben was making two prints of everything, so that, as he had promised, he could send one of each to Karl, on the West Coast.

This was, then, the last moving picture we would ever make together, I knew, and as Ben set the prints to dry, and as I continued to draw strips of film across the light—images of Laura staring down at Mister Gardner as if at a child suffering an incurable illness—I wanted to throw my arms around my uncle's neck, to tell him how sorry I was that I would soon be leaving. I wanted to tell him about the decision Gloria and I had reached the night before—Vito had beaten her again, and had threatened to beat the children too—when we had sealed our pact: that neither of us was allowed to even begin imagining what might happen to us after we left Fort Lee. Until we actually set out upon our journey west with the children, we would keep our new identities—who we were and where we were going and how we intended to survive—a secret, even from ourselves.

But I said nothing. Instead, I did what I always did when we worked together. I talked with Ben about ways we might arrange our pictures—about possible sequences—and about what colors might make the images softer or stronger, sweeter or more painful, more lyric or more harsh.

Did I ever tell you about the first movies I ever saw? he asked.

No.

They were like *tableaux vivants*, but they were performed not by living people upon a stage, but on a bedsheet nailed to the wall of a Second Avenue dance hall Karl and I used to go to, with the pictures projected onto the screen by a magic lantern. While the images appeared, a man would stand to one side, telling the story and acting out all the parts. I was eight or nine years old the first time I saw them—we called them "slow movies" — and I remember thinking that the man who created these stories was like God himself, for he seemed to know and to do everything: he sold the tickets, and put up the sheet, and set out the chairs. He changed the showcards, and worked the lantern, and put the music on the phonograph, and acted out the parts — and even though there were by count a mere four images per minute passing through the lantern, the images seemed to me to be forever in motion.

Is that when you decided you wanted to make moving pictures?

Maybe, he said.

Is that when you and Karl first began making plans for our studio?

I don't remember, he said, and I sensed that he was already regretting having given away some of his story. This was the way it always was with my parents and my uncles: they only told me stories when they chose to. Ben gestured to the bench, to indicate that there was still work to be done, but instead of obeying him, I asked if he and my mother were definite about their decision *not* to accept Karl's offer to move to California.

Yes, he said.

You never talk about your own mother, I said to him. I've often wondered about that — that neither you, nor Karl, nor my mother ever talk much about your mother, and about what happened to her. Would you tell me about her — about what happened to her?

Ben said nothing. He cut more film. I took the frames from him and pasted in a close-up of Laura's eyes in the moment before Mister Gardner kisses her — a close-up in which, looking down at her eyes, we see her look down, so that, following her gaze, our eyes are drawn to her lips. Less than twenty feet away, I knew, on opposite sides of the hallway, my father and mother were fast asleep in their separate bedrooms. No noise came from the street outside. It was no longer night, I sensed, though neither was it day.

Our story was complete, and even if I were to leave before we had placed all the images and titles where we wanted them, Ben, I knew, would do the rest of the cutting and splicing, after which he would, as he'd promised, send a copy to Karl.

This is what happened in our story:

A young woman, saved from suicide by a stranger, believes she has found true love, only to discover, as she is kept by the stranger, not only that he has kept women innumerable times before, but that the more indifferent and harsh he is to her, the more her love for him grows. What she comes to believe is this: that just as he was sent to save her from death, so she has been sent to save him from a fate worse than death—from the prison of an unloving heart.

Thus, when they kiss, her eyes close, not in submission, but in the knowledge that her heart has at last found an object worthy of its love. And when they kiss, his eyes open wide, not in triumph at yet another conquest, but in astonishment, for he feels what he has never before allowed himself to feel: the first stirrings of true kindness.

Although Laura may be imprisoned by Mister Gardner, he lives in a prison he himself has constructed—and the walls he has built to keep others from reaching his heart have only served, he begins to understand, to keep the slight movements of his own heart hidden from himself.

But if he changes now, what can he do about those acts he has already committed? And how can he feel worthy of Laura's love—of her forgiveness—if he cannot forgive himself?

Our story ends with Laura and Mister Gardner walking through the city until they arrive at the wharf where they first met. Here he opens his heart to her, telling her of how he has been responsible for the suffering of his wife and his children, and for the ruin of many women.

When he asks if she can ever forgive him, she kisses his brow, and to my surprise—for until we reached this moment in our story, neither I nor Ben knew this would occur—she shakes her head sideways and says she cannot. She leaves him there, on the spot where he first found her.

In a sequence we tinted indigo blue so that it would appear to be taking place at night, Mister Gardner writes a note of farewell, after which it is he, and not Laura, who slips into the darkness of the sea. From the black, rippled surface of the water we then dissolve to Laura's mirror. We watch her watching Mister Gardner's image as first his chin and his mouth, and then his nose and eyes and hair slowly fade and disappear.

I called our story *The Mirror of Love*, and in this final scene we moved from the darkness of Laura's eyes into the mirror's dark oval—the black cloth I had stared into, and upon which we had superimposed our images—that darkness wherein I had condemned Mister Gardner to non-existence, and within which, I now sensed, even after I was no longer living and working with Ben, I might be able to conjure up any story, feeling, or memory I would desire.

Sometime before dawn Ben tapped me on the shoulder. I sat up at once, apologizing for having fallen asleep.

Here, Ben said, and I followed him to his ground-glass screen, and looked at the images: Laura looking into the mirror and seeing Mister Gardner's image begin to fray and to vanish.

It's really quite wonderful, Ben said. I'll work on it some more—later today—but we've done well this time, Joey.

I rubbed sleep from my eyes. Ben handed me a glass of tea, into which I put a spoonful of raspberry jam.

I first met your father on the day we were supposed to see our mother, did you know that?

No.

Your mother had been seeing him for some time—she was not in love with him, she claimed, but she was flattered by his persistence—by the fact that, despite her protests, he continued to pursue her. Our own mother had stayed on the other side of the ocean because she was, once again, with child.

We had come here one at a time, you see. First Karl came, since he was the oldest, and when he made enough money, he sent for me, and then when Karl and I had saved enough money we sent for our mother and father. Our father came, but because our mother was with child again, they decided it was best for her to remain behind until she had given birth and the new child had passed its first birthday.

And so, when a year had passed, and the child—a girl named Bela Gittel—remained healthy, we sent money for their passage, and received word back that they had found a boat that would bring them to America.

When the day for the boat's landing arrived, we took a ferry across the river to New York City. It was a beautiful day in early June, I recall, and Simon accompanied us. Your mother claimed she had not invited him, but what was a girl to do when a guy wouldn't take no for an answer?

Karl and I, meeting your father for the first time, liked him. We may, in fact, have liked him more than your mother did, I've often thought. And our father did not disapprove. At any rate, when the boat arrived, neither our mother nor our sister was on it. We rented a small boat that took us out to Ellis Island, and we made inquiries, and every day after that, for the next several months, we continued to make inquiries. We sent letters across the sea to our mother, to cousins, to friends, to authorities.

And—?

Ben shrugged. Simon came to our house every day. Your mother wept, and Simon wiped away her tears and promised that he would care for her all the days of her life. We received verification that our mother and sister had left our village, yet from the time they made their farewells there until this morning, no other news of her, or of our sister, has ever come to us.

A year later, on the anniversary of the day they had not arrived, our father went to bed. I'll wait here, he said. Within three months, he died. Six weeks later your mother and Simon married, and less than a year after that, you were born.

When my father entered our room, carrying before him a tray upon which he had arranged our breakfasts, Ben and I were still at work.

Your friend is waiting, my father said.

My friend?

The young woman gives her name as Gloria.

My father set down the tray, looked to either side, and then, raising his eyebrows, he whispered in my ear: Oh, I have seen much sadness in my time, young man, but rarely have I seen a sadness such as that in this woman's eyes.

I tried to imagine a room where I might store the fragrance of our glue, along with the cool, silky feel of the film itself as, tinting it for a dawn scene of Laura and Mister Gardner, I had let it loop through an amber-colored bath. Gloria entered the room, but neither Marco nor Angelina were with her. She wore a large camel's hair coat, its collar turned up, a coat I recognized as Vito's.

I moved to her at once. Where are the children? I asked.

There's no time, she said. Come.

But we've finished our new picture, and I was hoping to show it to you.

I told you, there's no time.

Where are the children?

In the lake.

In the *lake*? But I don't understand. . . .

But you do, she said. So don't hand me crap now, Joey. Just get your stuff and let's get going.

And who are you, young woman? my father asked.

My name is Gloria Antonelli, she said. And soon I'll be so famous that even you won't be able to forget my name.

That would certainly be a miracle, my father said. Unless—tell me, please—you plan on becoming a movie star.

No, Gloria said. Because I'm gonna be more famous than a movie star. Actresses are gonna fight for the chance to make movies from *my* story.

I never forget a movie star I met, my father said. Once I kissed Miss Gish, did you know that?

What about Vito? I asked.

He went nuts the way he always does after he finishes a job for Carlo, telling me that if I didn't believe what he threatened to do to me—if I didn't do what he wanted, he would do stuff to the kids.

But he wouldn't, I said. You've told me a thousand times how much he loves the children.

Not any more he doesn't, Gloria said.

Gloria took my hand. Come on, she said. Just do what I say and save your questions for later.

My hand in hers, she led me into my bedroom and closed the door behind us.

Just don't say anything till I'm finished, she said as soon as we were alone. Because this is what happened, okay? He kept saying he would do stuff to the children—all this garbage I heard before, about poking their eyes out and cutting them up—but it was different this time because he saw that the suitcases were packed and figured things out pretty quick.

But—

Just listen, she said. So what happened was that while Carlo was here playing footsie with your mother to give himself an alibi, Vito was down in the meadowlands shoveling up blood and mud, and afterwards he got crazier than ever, imagining me and you together, because if I left him for a kid like you, he figured he'd be a laughing stock to everyone and that Carlo would pay somebody to do to him what he'd just done to somebody else. He started trying to slam me around, but I grabbed the children fast, got them into my bedroom, and locked the door, figuring he wouldn't hurt me again if they were there.

Oh yeah, she said. You let a guy piss in you for a few minutes and you pay the bill for the rest of your life. But I was still as big a fool as ever, right? Because he broke down the door and started in on the three of us anyway.

So that's when I did it, and that's what you're gonna read in the newspapers tomorrow, she said, and she described an arc in the air with her hand, as if the headline she recited were there: *First She Kills Her Husband And Then She Drowns Their Children.*

When I went to her, I expected her to fight me and push me away, the look in her eyes was so wild, but when I put my arms around her, she collapsed at once, as if a rod inside her had broken, and held to me.

Tell me it's not true, I said.

It's not true, she said.

I mean it, I said. Please—?

You told me to tell you it wasn't true, so I did. What more do you want?

I don't believe you, I said.

Yeah, she said. Me neither. Only what bothers me most isn't what I did to Vito, but that I used the children. I *used* them, don't you see, Joey? I used them to protect me when my job is to protect them.

The collar of her coat fell away slightly, and I saw an open gash that ran along the edge of her jaw. I reached out to touch the clotted blood, but she pushed my hand away.

Listen hey, she said, we ain't got time because while Vito's growing cold, Carlo's gonna be getting hot. As soon as he finds Vito he's gonna take after me, and that means he's gonna take after you too.

Gloria opened my suitcase, dumped my regular clothes from it and told me to bring her my makeup kit, along with the wigs and clothing I'd been using to play Laura.

When we left my room, my father was waiting for us. Setting out to seek your fortune, I'll bet, he said. Well, you certainly are a brave young man. He tapped on the side of my suitcase with his knuckles. Good-bye and good luck to you two young people.

Where's Ben? I asked.

My father set his violin on his shoulder, began playing Brahms' "Lullaby."

Come, Gloria said. I looked back, toward Ben's room,

then walked outside. On the roof of our building, my mother, her veil copper-colored in the morning sun, was sitting beneath her beach umbrella the way she did at the start of each day. She lifted the brim of her white summer hat and looked down at me.

Well, she said. Did you think I didn't know you would leave me too? But it's all right, because when I think of your father I recall what my own father used to say—that a man is like a tree because he dies from the top down.

Simon, she called. Oh Simon!

Here I am, my father replied, and he appeared beside her, on the roof.

I'm quite hungry this morning, my mother said to him. So I hope breakfast is ready.

On the northern bank of the lake, the children's clothes were set out upon a low, moss-covered rock.

The way I look at it is this, Gloria said. Where's the fun in killing people you don't know? This way, with me and Vito and the children, I kept it in the family.

You're lying, I said. I know it. I can tell from your eyes— from the way they're laughing. You're lying.

Ah, Joey, it's the old story, don't you understand? she said. Sure. If I can't have them, then *nobody* can. That's what I'll say in court—that I knew I'd get the chair for killing my husband, but that it was my love for my children that made me do it. She pressed her hands to her heart and, as if she were playing herself in a moving picture, she spoke: "If I cannot have them, then nobody else can either!"

Stop it, I said. Please—

Wouldn't that be a great line, though, for when they make a moving picture from my life?

Then she laughed and put her arm around my shoulder and told me she didn't want to drive me totally nuts. This is what's really going to happen next, okay? she said. I'm turning myself in and you're getting out of here. Because if you don't, I'll wind up hurting more people than I planned.

She drew me to her and kissed me on the mouth. Her lips were warm. Then she was running up the hill toward the spot where I had stood a few years before, when I had watched the Leskos cutting out cakes of ice. I heard voices—my name—and I turned. A voice called to me again and I realized it was coming from the ice house.

When I opened the door to the ice house, Angelina rushed into my arms.

Surprise! she yelled. *Surprise!*

Marco was sitting on the floor, putting clothespins into a milk bottle, one by one.

I heard Gloria laugh, and I turned around. She stood in the doorway, hands on hips, grinning broadly.

I mean, what kind of girl did you take me for anyway? she asked.

I held Angelina, pressed her cheek to mine.

I mean, did you think I could ever really do you-know-what to my own kids?

I didn't think, I said. I just . . .

Same old Joey, she said. But here's something that'll really bring tears to your eyes.

She reached inside her jacket, took out an envelope, handed it to me and showed me what was inside: a thick stack of bills—fives, tens, twenties.

But where—?

Let's just call it a going-away present from Carlo and the boys. So you listen up now, okay? You leave the clothes down by the lake where I put them—I threw some other stuff from the kids into the water, so they'll believe I did what I'm gonna tell them I did, and with the cold weather coming on soon, and all the snappers they got at the bottom here, they're not gonna look for long or wonder too much. But they'll never find any bodies either, which will help me stay alive for a while. In the meantime, you get started on the trip with the kids, like we planned.

But—?

You get started—I'll catch up later.

But how—?

You leave that to me.

You'll really join us? It's a promise?

Cross my heart.

Mommy always keeps her promises, Angelina said.

Gloria bent down, tucked a few locks of Angelina's hair under her wool bonnet.

And what's your name, Gloria asked, forever and ever now?

Regina.

That's right. And what's your brother's name?

Marvin.

And what about your Uncle Joey?

Angelina giggled. We'll call him Mommy, she said.

You're some smart girl, Gloria said. So tell me again—what will you do every night before you go to sleep?

Pray-to-God-to-be-good.

Gloria kissed Angelina, lifted the baby—Marco was not yet a year old—kissed him on the lips, then set him back on the floor.

So you take good care of them for me, she said.

Of course, I said. Only—

Only nothing.

Before I could find words, Gloria's arms were around me, her small chest heaving against my own. I was surprised, holding her close to me, to discover she was so thin—that her body was still like that of a young girl.

Then she was gone. I lifted Marco, who gurgled happily, and I touched my lips to the soft indentation on top of his head. Angelina took my hand and we walked outside and watched Gloria climb the hill.

Wave good-bye, I said.

Angelina waved good-bye.

Hey Joey! Gloria called, when she had reached the top of the hill.

What?

You don't forget to have a good time, yeah?

1924

I sat with my back to our stove, and while Regina stood on a chair beside me brushing out my hair, I pictured Eddie walking from his house to mine, crossing the small footbridge that spanned the Menomonee River, and I wondered what it might be like to *be* Eddie— what it might be like to live a life in which the expectation of seeing me could make someone else happy.

Please hurry, I said. I don't want to be late.

You won't be late, Regina said. And I know you, Mommy. You always get nervous before Eddie comes here.

I went to the window, wiped away a circle of frost with the back of my hand. Below, the street was deserted. I glanced in the small mirror nailed to the wall above the sink. Because our room was so cold, it had taken longer than usual for my hair to dry, and the ends were still damp.

I sat, and Regina climbed onto the chair and began brushing my hair again.

I hope I have hair that's as beautiful as yours when I grow up, she said.

You will, I said.

As long and as silky?

You're going to be a very beautiful woman some day.

Really?

Really.

As beautiful as you?

At least.

And if I'm beautiful, will I be happy too?

Very.

You always say the same things, Regina said.

So do you, I said.

So do *you*, she said, and we both laughed.

Then I closed my eyes, and drifted into a darkness sweeter than sleep. Except for the hissing of steam from the tea kettle, and the flapping of the shade, where, despite all I'd done to seal off the window, the winds coming off Lake Michigan still sliced their way through, our room was without sound.

Later, her mouth close to my ear, Regina blew softly at the hairs on my neck.

Does that tickle? she asked.

A little bit.

But you like it when I blow on you like this, don't you?

Yes.

I have a secret question for you.

She moved closer so that her lips touched my ear. Is Eddie going to ask you to marry him tonight? she whispered.

I heard her scream, saw her leap down from the chair, saw the brush fly into the air.

I told you never never to ask me that! I shouted. *Didn't I—?*

Please don't be angry with me, Regina said. She grabbed the hairbrush, clutched it to her chest. It's just that you look so beautiful tonight, with your hair and your uniform, and—

Be quiet, I said.

Don't hit me again, Regina said, and she crawled backwards along the floor, her forearm across her eyes. I'll do anything you want, only please don't hit me again.

I didn't hit you, I said.

Yes you did, she said. You always say you don't, but you do.

Where's Marvin? I asked.

I don't know.

I pulled her arm away from her face. You look at me when I talk to you, young lady. Where *is* he?

You're hurting me, she said.

Tell me.

I don't know, and I don't care either, she said. I don't care and I don't know and I wish he was dead.

Me too, I wanted to say.

I let go of her arm, closed my eyes to stop the room from spinning, and imagined myself adrift in a small boat on Lake Michigan, the boat rising and falling in the ice-cold swells. Regina had retreated to the pantry.

You come out at once and help me look for your brother, I said. I'm going to count to three.

I heard Regina sniffle. You didn't say the magic word, she said.

Please come out, I said. I'll start counting now. One . . .

Regina came out. I'll find him, she said.

She wiped her eyes and nose with the back of her hand. I offered her my handkerchief, but she pushed it away, and held her nose.

He did it again, she said. I knew it. He did it again and if I step in it I'll kill him.

She pointed to the far end of our room, to the space where, behind a thin curtain—a floral print in black, green and gold, of parrots and moonflowers—I slept at night.

I drew back the curtain. Marvin, with no clothes on, was seated in the middle of my pillow like a young prince.

Phooey! Regina exclaimed. He did it all over your bed this time.

Marvin held one of my nail files in his fist and was jabbing the point of the file into the back of his hand.

Do something, Mommy, Regina said. Please. Don't just stand there. *Do* something.

You're right, I said. I should do something.

I moved toward Marvin, but he slipped down into the space between my bed and the wall. I took him by the wrist, pulled him up, held him high in the air, careful to keep his body from touching mine so he wouldn't soil my uniform. I carried him across the room, set him down in the sink.

You've been a bad boy, I said. Do you know that? You've been a very bad boy again.

I held both his wrists with one hand, pressed them against the porcelain ledge below the mirror, then tucked the towel I'd been using to dry my hair into my collar, and washed out the pitted wounds on the back of his hand.

Regina had pushed a chair to the sink and was caressing Marvin's cheek. He grinned, then swirled sideways and snapped at her hand with his teeth. I saw blood spurt, drip down along his chin.

You let go, I commanded. You let go at once.

Marvin did what I said. Regina held her finger in the air, but she didn't cry out.

I held Marvin in place while Regina washed her finger under the faucet. The punctures, I saw, were not deep.

Put some iodine on, and wrap it. Then go and fetch Loretta. Eddie will be here any minute, and I don't want him to see us like this.

I'll clean up your bed first, Regina said.

No, I said. You'll only make it worse. Just do what I say. But yes—my bed—all right—only first clean up Marvin's mess and tend to your hand. Then go and fetch Loretta.

If I do, do you promise you won't hurt him? Regina asked.

I promise.

Cross your heart and hope to die?

Yes.

Say it.

Cross my heart and hope to die.

Regina sat on the braided rug beside the stove. She dabbed iodine on her finger, wrapped the finger in gauze. Her movements were remarkably deliberate and exact. She pulled the gauze tight, snipped it with scissors, cut off a small rectangle of adhesive tape, and sealed the bandage.

I washed Marvin with warm water and soap, dried him

with a bath towel, then went to the window again, lifted the shade, and saw that Eddie was at the far end of the street.

There were still things to do. I had to clean myself, and to dress Marvin, and to clear my bed and sprinkle it with perfume. I had to make sure Regina's finger was all right, to draw my curtain closed, to put more wood in the stove, to set out supper for the children, to give Loretta her instructions . . . and there was no time. There was no time, and then I would be gone, and then I would return and they would be sleeping or pretending sleep, and Loretta would want to talk about them, and I would pay her, and she would leave, and I would lie down, and after three or four hours of sleep, I would wake, and everything would begin all over again. I would wash them, and cook for them, and feed them. I would take them to the toilet, and tend to their needs, and dress them, and break up their fights, and dress Marvin for going outside, and take Regina to school, and return, and undress Marvin, and change him, and clean him, and wash our clothes and hang them out over the stove and clean the toilet and make our beds and try to rest, but by then it would be time to do the shopping, and to fetch Regina, to come back home, to cook and clean and wash dishes and pots and make supper, and prepare myself for going to the theater.

I don't see why we *need* Loretta, Regina said. She's just an old dumb Indian, and what good would she be if anything happened to us?

You are not to talk that way about Loretta, I said.

But she *is* stupid, Regina said. She can't even read or write her own name and I could take care of Marvin better than her. I'm old enough.

Stop talking, I said.

It's *you*, Regina continued. It's your going away that makes him crazy.

I said to stop talking. Why must you talk so much?

Regina put a finger to her lips, and when she did, Marvin imitated her.

I had not yet drawn lines around my eyes, or chosen my

lipstick, or pinned my hair so that it would sit properly under my cloak during the walk to the theater. Mister Fehr, the theater's owner, loved my hair—it was the reason I had been given the job, I knew—and if I wanted to retain my position, my hair had to be soft and silky so that, admiring it each evening when it was time for inspection, Mister Fehr would whisper endearments to me in German.

I let Regina help me dress Marvin, clean off my bed, and sprinkle perfume, and set the foul-smelling linens in the bucket outside our room, next to the lavatory. Then I outlined my eyes with liner, emphasizing the lower lids so that I would seem to be as old as I claimed I was. On the back of my hand I drew light marks with three different lipsticks, and, as was our custom, I let Regina choose the shade she thought best. I did my lips, and then I did Regina's, which she loved, and while she went downstairs to fetch Loretta, I pinned up my hair and set out the supper I'd prepared earlier in the day: beef and barley soup, Kaiser rolls, raspberry jam, chocolate pudding, milk.

Each evening, after I'd completed my duties in the Alhambra's checkroom, I would take up my post at the foot of the Western Staircase in the Grand Foyer, and, while Eddie called out, "For the best remaining seats, kindly take the staircase to your left! For the best remaining seats, ladies and gentlemen, kindly take the staircase to your left!," I would direct people toward these seats, and—my particular assignment—help elderly men and women make their way up the staircase if they preferred not to ride in the elevator. When the community sing and stage presentations were over, and the front doors and cashiers' windows had been closed for the night, I'd leave my station in the Grand Foyer, and ascend to the balcony in time to watch the orchestra descend on its platform.

Mister and Mrs. Purseglove, our organists, would play their final chords, and, bathed in rose spotlights, they too would descend below stage level into the orchestra pit, after which the enormous curtains, below the swags and furbelows, would draw closed. Then, as the lights dimmed, the curtains would open again—the silver screen, bordered in black velvet, would by now have been lowered—but I would find myself looking, not at the stage, where the thin scrims that hung in front of the screen were parting for the showing of the newsreel, travelogue, or whatever else preceded our feature presentation that night, but upwards, to where—as if the theater was open to the heavens—soft billowing clouds drifted by, thousands of stars twinkled, and comets streaked one after the other across a vast and infinite void.

No matter how difficult my day had been, I felt, once I was inside the theater, and especially in this moment, I was happy. I would gaze up at the make-believe heavens and, during the hush that preceded the first notes the organs would play as prelude to the moving pictures, I'd find myself engaged in imaginary conversations with Gloria, telling her about her children, and of all that was happening in their lives.

On this night, however, just as I'd started to tell her about how Regina had helped me tend to Marvin, Eddie touched my arm.

Dreaming about me again? he asked.

I smiled, but said nothing.

You had some swell look on your face before you knew I was here watching you, he said. He touched the swagger stick to his heart, and told me again how beautiful I was.

You really shouldn't talk to me this way, I said. You can get into trouble if someone hears you. And if Mister Fehr should find out . . .

I don't care, Joanna, he said. Because you're the sun and moon and stars to me, and the danger of getting caught—well, that just makes me more determined than ever to win your heart.

I turned away, toward the screen, upon which a young couple was riding in a streetcar, and while Eddie continued to pay court to me, I heard my Uncle Ben's voice, reciting some of his rules: Never to shoot close-ups against white or a moving background. Never to crank fast against moving water. Never to put rouge on your cheeks unless, since red photographed black, you wanted them to appear dark and hollow. And never ever to let your head drop lower than the key light, or it would age your features without mercy.

Eddie moved closer to me, his arm rubbing against mine.

Hey, are those tears I see in your eyes? he asked. I didn't say the wrong thing, did I?

No, I said. You're fine, Eddie. Only . . .

Only what?

Only this can never be—you and me—and not for any reasons you can know.

Hey, he said. I never felt like this about anyone. You ask anybody, Joanna, and they'll tell you what a restless guy I've been most of my life. But when it comes to you, I can be the most patient man in the world.

I am not who you think I am, I said. If you knew the truth about me, you would feel differently.

If I knew the truth? Eddie said. He tapped on his chest again. What's going on in here is the only truth I'm listening to these days.

Oh Eddie, I said. I don't want to lead you on. You should find a woman worthier of you than me.

Eddie moved close to me and told me he would be the one to decide whether or not he was worthy of me. I looked at the young couple on the screen—they were at an amusement park—and I saw the words I was thinking, as if on a printed card Ben was setting on his easel, so that we could photograph it:

ALONE WITH HER SECRET

SHE LEAVES A TRAIL OF BROKEN HEARTS
MILWAUKEE, FEBRUARY, 1924

Eddie was twenty-eight years old and had served in the War. He had been gassed and left for dead on a battlefield in

Normandy, yet had returned and, after fifteen months in hospitals, to the surprise of his doctors, had recovered fully. He was the eldest of nine children, and lived with his family at the north end of the city, near the Nash Auto Works, where his father, uncles, and his four brothers worked in the foundry and machine shops there.

He tucked his bugle under his arm, whispered to me that the reason he'd been able to get away from his duties was that Mister Fehr wanted to see me in his office, and that he'd been told to escort me there.

But who'll guard my station while I'm gone?

He said he'd already assigned another usherette to take my place, and the usherette, a slender German girl named Eva Bornstein, emerged from the darkness below, and approached us.

I smiled at once, for Eva was, I thought, the most beautiful young woman I'd ever known—with thick strawberry-blond curls, and large, pale blue-green eyes. She was not yet seventeen years old, and she lived with her family only a short walk from Eddie's home. Her father and three older brothers also worked at the Nash Auto Works.

Congratulations, she said to me, and she kissed me once on each cheek. I'm very happy for you, Joanna.

I nodded, though I did not understood what she was talking about.

When you're rich and famous, I hope you won't forget me, she said, and she pulled me to her and kissed me on the lips.

Oh forgive me, Joanna, she exclaimed. Please forgive me—but I am just so happy for you!

I felt my knees go weak, and when Eva kissed me a second time, I threw my arms around her neck and kissed her back. When she pulled away and told me that I deserved all the happiness that would soon be mine, I kissed once more, so that, through our wool blazers and frilled blouses, I might feel her small heart beating against my own.

Eddie said that we shouldn't make Mister Fehr wait any

longer, and so, following the glow of Eddie's swagger stick, I let him lead me back down to the Grand Foyer, where, when they saw Eddie, the other ushers came to attention and saluted.

Everyone was congratulating me and, as we walked across the enormous oval rug that covered the rotunda's marble floor, a rug brilliant with forests of swirling green, gold, and pink peacocks, tamarisks, and sultans—I looked up to where, in the overhead dome, a golden dragon held in its claws a large crystal chandelier, and I found myself imagining that the dragon was holding me upside down by the ankles and that I was swinging back and forth across the Grand Foyer, from one side to the other, holding Marvin and Regina upside down by *their* ankles, the two of them shrieking with joy.

We left the foyer, moved past picture galleries, lounges, and the infirmary, past the nursery where, for matinees, mothers could leave their children, and up another carpeted staircase, one whose newel posts were carved elephants from whose bejeweled backs rose high winged columns in which were set white globed lanterns that lit the way for people ascending and descending.

Eddie stopped, and whispered the news that Mister Fehr had chosen me to be his designated companion on the night, two weeks hence—the evening of Saint Valentine's Day—when Mister S. L. Rothafel, the illustrious Roxy himself, would make his long-awaited visit to our theater.

No! I said. It cannot be.

But it is, Eddie said. You're it, Joanna, and even though it breaks my heart to think of you all dolled up for that stingy Kraut bastard, I want you to know that having you picked out for this honor makes me the proudest guy in Milwaukee.

Oh no, Eddie, I said. No, no. . . .

Ah, it's okay, Eddie said. I mean, maybe I wish I had the bucks to treat you the way guys like them can treat a girl—but I'm not jealous is what I'm trying to say.

You don't know anything, I said.

I know I love you, he declared.

That's what I mean, I said. If you love me and think you know me, then you don't know anything.

But my words only encouraged Eddie. He told me of the plans he'd gone over with Mister Fehr: for a gala dinner, and for opening night of the new stage show Roxy was bringing with him, and for the Sunday night radio show Roxy would send out across the nation the way he did each week, but from the Alhambra this time, and about the new moving picture they were bringing, which would open at the Alhambra even before it was shown in New York City.

Take me back to my station, I said.

We were at the landing of the first balcony, and Eddie drew me with him into the darkness just outside one of the belvederes. The organs were blasting away with music for a chase scene, and the audience—more than three thousand men and women—was laughing the way audiences did in those days, as if, in that moment, they'd forgotten that any unhappiness might ever be visited upon them again. I stared at the cream and buff plaster that circled around us in rib-boned courses, twisting upwards along columns, walls, and cornices, into domes and minarets, winged griffins, smiling cherubs, turbaned caliphs, and crimson firebirds, and I felt faint.

Eddie touched my forehead, put a hand in the small of my back to steady me. You just take it easy for a few minutes and you'll be fine, he said. You're not scared of being alone with Mister Fehr, are you? Because if either him or Roxy try anything funny with you, believe you me, they're gonna have Eddie Kucharski to reckon with!

It's not seeing Mister Fehr that frightens me, I said.

Then what?

I looked away, watched dim amber exit lights flutter across the plush carpeting as if the lights were under water, and I realized that I was imagining myself walking across a meadow with Eva, the two of us holding hands, then lying down on the grass.

Sometimes I don't understand you at all, Eddie said. He took my hands in his. But whatever it is that's making you feel this way, it doesn't matter, because I'm here to tell you that I love you no matter what.

I nodded.

I didn't go too far, before, the things I said to you, did I? he asked. I mean, it's one thing to love somebody, but when it turns out you also like and admire the person—hey, that's as good as it gets.

I felt heat drain from my cheeks and lips, and I wondered how I would ever be able to tell Eddie what he least suspected: which was that I knew Roxy and had often visited him in New York City with my mother, father, and uncles when he was in charge of theaters there—that he knew of the double-roles I played in our moving pictures and of my disappearance at the time of Gloria's arrest, and that he might recognize me. And this only meant that, yet again, I would have to flee with the children to another city where I would have to find a new place for us to live, and new work for myself.

I'm tired, I said. I get tired sometimes.

Shh, he said, and he stroked my hair. Shh.

I let my head rest against his chest, and I took pleasure in listening to him tell me what I wanted to hear: that everything would be all right, and that he loved me and would never stop loving me, no matter what.

I lifted my head from his chest, and in the dim light, with the faint red glow of the swagger stick lighting his face from below, the tiny scar that ran from the crevice of his chin to the right corner of his lip seemed to pulse slightly. I touched his lips with my gloved hand and I knew that I felt, in this moment, not unlike the young woman he believed I was.

When he told me again that he didn't give one hoot for how and where some other man had fathered my children, and when his lips were inches from my eyes so that I felt as if I were reading the words he was speaking to me, I felt, too, a most pleasurable stirring in my groin, and had I not reminded myself in that moment of who I truly was, I might not have been able to resist the sweet desire I had to let him press his lips against mine and to tell him I was truly his.

After Mister Fehr finished telling me about Roxy's visit, and of the festivities associated with it, and after he told me, again, of how he first met Roxy a decade before, on a train from Minneapolis, and that it was Roxy himself who talked him into transforming the Alhambra into a theater that could be made to pay—that the secret lay in adding moving pictures to the theatrical bills—and after he told me once more of the time Sarah Bernhardt sat where I was now sitting, and allowed him to kiss her hand, and said to him, *Monsieur Fehr, vous irez loin*, Mister Fehr asked if he might have the honor of kissing *my* ungloved hand.

Mister Fehr backed me up against his grand piano, whispering rapidly in German, telling me I was his little *schnecken*, that there was no reason to be shy with him—what was a kiss upon an ungloved hand, after all?—and while, to buy time, I whispered back, "Not here, kind sir! Not here!", Eddie reappeared, clicking his heels, and announcing, "Eddie Kucharski reporting—is it time to escort Miss Joanna back to her station?"

Mister Fehr let go of me.

My hero, I whispered to Eddie.

Eddie grinned. Mister Fehr turned away, opened a cabinet and poured himself a drink. He said there was no need for either of us to hurry away—it was *his* theater, after all—and he wanted me to see the new moving picture so that I could talk about it knowledgeably with Mister Rothafel.

Come, children, he said, and he led us from his office, past his private bath and reception room, and into a small, elegantly decorated theater, where he threaded film into a projector. As the credits appeared, he told us to imagine that the Alhambra orchestra was playing the Holy Grail motif from Wagner's *Parsifal*.

I looked to the screen, where a fluttering rectangle of

white light appeared. Mister Fehr sat beside me and told me I had nothing to fear from him except the gratitude he owed me for having agreed to be his queen.

Eddie whispered that if Mister Fehr tried anything, he would knock his block off.

Words appeared on the screen:

ADOLPH ZUKOR PRESENTS

THE SECRET OF LOVE
A Film by Karl S. Davidoff

Although I'd seen my uncle's name on the screen many times before, when I saw it this time, I gasped. Eddie and Mister Fehr turned to me so swiftly that they nearly bumped foreheads. I pushed them away and stood, and I may have said *No!* or I may have said *Yes!*, or I may have said nothing at all. Blood swirled inside my head with such force that when I fixed my eyes upon the image on the screen—a woman gazing into an oval mirror—I knew only that this image became the last one I saw.

When I opened my eyes, Eva smiled down at me.

Where am I? I asked.

In the infirmary, Eva said.

The infirmary? I closed my eyes, opened them again, and Eva was still there. Then I'm not in paradise? I said.

I heard harps and felt myself floating upwards, through clouds and past stars. I tried to raise my hand, so that I might touch Eva's lips, so that I might draw her face down to mine.

I love you, I said.

Eva laughed, and spoke to others. She's fine, she said.

I tried to sit up, but Eva pushed me down gently. Her head seemed to hover within a world of gently falling snowflakes.

Don't move, she said. You've had a great shock.

But I love you, I said again.

Shh, she said, and she bent over me—her shadow blocking out all else—and pressed lips that tasted of roses and honey against my own.

I love you too, she whispered. But be good now.

Eddie's head appeared beside Eva's. Then Mister Fehr's head appeared. Eddie asked if I was all right. Had I eaten supper before coming to work? Had the children kept me awake all night? Mrs. Strom's head appeared—Mrs. Strom was our head nurse at the Alhambra—and she inserted a thermometer in my mouth. Eddie was explaining to Mister Fehr that perhaps the strain of working while raising two small children had driven me to exhaustion.

Eva held my hand and said that Mister Fehr had been kind enough to let her leave work early in order to accompany me home. Mrs. Strom held my other hand. She announced that my pulse was a bit rapid, but that I had no fever.

Perhaps, Mister Fehr suggested, it was the movie itself that had caused me such upset. This had happened in his theater many times, after all—did we not recall the many women who had fainted during showings of *House of Bondage* and *Damaged Goods*? Could Mrs. Strom forget how crowded the infirmary became when *Birth of a Nation* and *The Wind* had played?

Nothing can move people the way moving pictures can move people! he stated. Nothing in the world!

Mister Fehr's head appeared now, behind Eva's. Grinning broadly, he begged my forgiveness. Then Eddie's head appeared, and then Mrs. Strom's head appeared, and their three heads seemed to rotate slowly around Eva's head, like flesh-covered moons.

Well, my child, Mister Fehr said. I certainly do not wish to frighten you, yet I do wish to know one thing, and it is this: Am I not right about the power of the moving picture?

You're right, I said.

Ah, Mister Fehr said. He came closer to me, lowered his voice. And tell me this—tell me what it was in this story that so frightened you, dear child. Was it the image in the mirror?

Yes.

But why?

I don't know, I said, except that when I saw the man's face there, everything else vanished.

Remarkable, Mister Fehr said.

What man? Eddie asked.

Mister Fehr turned to the others and spoke: I knew I had chosen well, he said, but I did not know how wisely.

Mister Fehr walked in a circle around my bed. Our darling Joanna saw the man in the mirror, he said. Did you hear? Did you *hear*—?

What man? Eddie asked. It was a *woman* looking into the mirror, not a man.

Aha! Mister Fehr said. You are right, my friend—it *was* a woman now, but afterwards, you see, it will *be* a man. Soon, when the woman looks in her mirror, she will see not herself but a man with whom she will fall in love. A man who will threaten to destroy her life!

Wow, Eddie said.

And why is this so? Mister Fehr went on. How is it that our darling Joanna has somehow known this ahead of time? I will tell you. Our darling Joanna has known this because of the power of the unseen and the unspoken to work upon us even when we do not know it is doing so! Once again, as Roxy has predicted, we see living proof of why the moving picture is the mightiest art form ever invented by the mind of man.

That's really terrific—that you guessed what was going to happen, Eddie said.

And its phenomenal success, in my opinion, Mister Fehr went on, is also due to the fact that with our moving picture theaters we have created magical palaces in which anyone— *anyone at all*—can afford to spend a few hours. We have created rooms with windows that allow you to look into other people's lives in any time, and in any place, and without them knowing it.

Come, Eva said to me. Let's go home.

I sat up, set my feet upon the floor. Eva wrapped a cloak

around my shoulders. Eddie said that he'd summoned a horse and carriage for us. Given the ferocity of the winds blowing in from Lake Michigan, the ride would be smoother and warmer in a carriage than in an automobile, he explained. He'd already given instructions to the driver to warm the blankets and light the foot braziers.

I stood, leaned upon Eva's arm.

But there is yet more good news, Mister Fehr said to me. So stay a moment more, my child. Stay. For I will now disclose to you a secret millions of Americans will come to know only after Roxy arrives here—a secret Roxy revealed to me yesterday.

Please, I said. No more good news.

Mrs. Strom cautioned Mister Fehr against shocking me again, and Eddie urged him to honor my request, but Mister Fehr dismissed them with a sweep of his hands.

The woman you have seen tonight in the moving picture, he declared, is not a woman but a man. Yes, my friends— she is both hero *and* heroine in this film, just as Mary Pickford was hero and heroine in *Stella Maris* and *Little Lord Fauntleroy*—but with a significant difference. And what is the difference? The difference is that nobody yet knows who this woman is, or *where* she is. The difference is that this woman, as Roxy has so aptly named her, is the true Mystery Woman herself.

Eva's arm circled my waist and kept me from falling.

When Roxy arrives here a fortnight hence, Mister Fehr continued, he will announce a competition that will award a grand prize of ten thousand dollars to that citizen who can discover who this Mystery Woman is.

Ten thousand dollars?! Eddie said.

The winner will travel to New York City to appear on a radio broadcast with Roxy and his gang, and, let us hope, with The Mystery Woman herself. Roxy is preparing advertisements to herald the search, and—thus our great, good fortune—all of this will begin here in the Alhambra.

Mister Fehr took my hands in his own and kissed them.

Does that not make you happy, my child? To be the queen who, at my side, will welcome Roxy here on Valentine's Day?

I said nothing.

Mister Fehr backed away and imitated the voice, familiar to us all, with which Roxy closed his radio broadcast each Sunday evening: "Good night," Mister Fehr said. "Pleasant dreams . . . God bless you. . . ."

Mister Fehr blew me a kiss, bowed, turned, and exited from the infirmary.

When we entered my room, I saw that Loretta was fast asleep in a chair beside the stove, and that, sucking away madly, Marvin's mouth was fastened to her breast.

I broke from Eva's grasp, tried to strike Marvin's face with my open hand, but he was too quick for me, and he slipped swiftly down from Loretta's lap, and scurried under the sink.

I screamed at Loretta that I had forbidden her to nurse Marvin, but she only smiled sleepily and told me not to fret. A child could never get too much loving, she said, and then she rambled on about what a fine young mother I was, and about what wonderful children Regina and Marvin were.

Marvin climbed up onto his bed, and onto Regina's lap, and glared at me. I heard a noise coming from under the sink, and saw a small rat chewing on a candle. I grabbed the bread knife from the kitchen table, hacked at the rat, but, like Marvin, it too was quicker than I was so that the knife's blade clanged loudly against one of the sink's pipes.

Marvin and Regina laughed. Loretta took the knife from my hand, set it back on the table and told me she'd brought the children corn pudding, greens, and taffy gum, and that they'd eaten well. Afterwards, she said, Regina had read stories to the three of them. Regina was the smartest girl in Milwaukee, she said. She was smarter than Houdini.

Loretta said that the reason Marvin was such a strong young boy was because of her milk. She pointed to my chest, said that God had not endowed me with the means to give

Marvin what he needed, so God had sent her to help us. I once nursed Houdini too, Loretta said—a fact she repeated each time she came to our room—and look where he is now.

Joanna was taken ill at the theater, Eva said to Loretta, and so they asked me to take her home. I'll stay with her to make sure she gets to sleep.

Let me pay you, I said to Loretta.

Loretta said she wouldn't take money from a sick woman.

I said I'll pay you, I said.

Loretta ignored me, and kissed the children good night.

Let me pay you, goddamn it! I screamed.

Loretta clucked inside her mouth, said that she did worry about how angry I got sometimes.

Regina and Marvin climbed back onto the bed, slipped under the covers together. Marvin stuck his thumb in his mouth, closed his eyes.

I heard the door close. Loretta was gone.

I sat on my bed. Eva went to the children, spoke with them, and returned to me.

They'll be fast asleep in no time, she said.

She drew the curtain closed.

Alone at last! she said. Then, as if she were a blind woman trying to determine what I looked like, she ran her hands slowly over my face.

Her fingers touched my throat, and played with the buttons of my blouse. I drew back.

No! I said. Please . . .

What is it? she asked. Aren't you happy to have me here?

I'm frightened, I said. And I'm cold. I must have caught a chill. I'll sleep in my clothing tonight. Just put the blankets over me.

Eva removed my shoes, one at a time. She said she had seen Houdini when he came to the Alhambra four years before, and that she had nearly fainted when she watched him being lowered, in chains and a straitjacket, into a tank of water. Her father claimed to have grown up with Houdini in Appleton, and to have helped defend him in fights on the way to and from school. She asked if I believed Loretta, about nursing Houdini.

I'm tired, I said. And you need to get home. The carriage is waiting for you—the children will wake up, and—

Eva laughed. Dear Joanna, she said. I sent the carriage on its way, and the children are asleep, and I've been waiting for this moment just as you have.

Her face was directly above mine, her eyes like slivers of transparent emerald, while her skin, when she took my hands and led them to her face, felt as if it might burst into flames.

Kiss me again, she said. Oh kiss me, Joanna. Kiss me the way you kissed me in the theater. *Please!*

I turned my head to the side, but Eva put her hand over my mouth. Then she took me by the chin, turned my face upwards again, and lowered her face to mine.

But what if the children should wake? I asked.

Who *cares* about the children, she said.

But we *can't*—! I protested.

Ah, but we can, she replied. Why not? I want to kiss you, Joanna. Nobody has ever kissed me the way you kissed me.

Then her lips were upon my lips—hot, smooth, deliciously sweet. I tried to get away, but she held my face with both hands now, one hand on my jaw, the other at the back of my neck.

I need air, I said. Please! I need air!

Golly, Joanna—isn't this the bee's knees? she said. Who would have thought? I mean, feel how *hot* I am. Just *feel!* Just feel the way my heart's pounding for you.

She took my hand and pressed it against her bosom.

I used to practice kissing with some of my girl cousins, she said, but kissing with them never did anything to me like this.

Then, before I realized what she was doing, my hand was being pressed against something softer and smoother than silk could ever be.

Rub me gently, she said. Oh Joanna, rub me gently. But slowly, very slowly. . . .

Her mouth was upon mine again, but without force, and I was frightened, not that the children would wake, but that Eva might discover how greatly I myself had awakened. So I did what she asked of me, and rubbed her breasts while she licked my neck, sucked on my lips, and chewed on my ears.

Gee whiz, she said, when, sometime later, she stopped. Who would have dreamt? I mean, you make me as crazy as a nun in a candle factory. I am *so* wet. I am just *so* wet.

She sat up, touched herself, then touched my mouth with fingers that tasted so sour they were sweet, and whispered that we could do anything we wanted—*anything at all!*—and that nobody would ever know.

Tell me what you want me to do for you, she whispered. Come on. Tell me. Tell me what *you* want.

I want to be somewhere else, I said.

Me too, she said. She traced the whorl of my ear with her tongue. But what else—come on—what else?

I want to *be* somebody else.

Okay then—how about if you be me and I be you? Would you like that?

Yes. Oh yes, I said. Only I just don't know why you or anybody else could ever care for me. I never *do* anything, and . . .

You not do anything?! she said. But you raise your children all by yourself—and that's the best work in the whole wide world!

But you don't understand, I said. You don't know.

I know the way you kiss, she said. I know that when I'm with you, I'm happy. So come on—tell me. Tell me what else you want. Tell me what you *really* want.

I don't know, I said, and I felt myself becoming so engorged, below, that I was frightened I was going to explode. I don't know anything at all. I don't know anything . . .

Shh, she said. Take it easy, okay? God—you're really upset, aren't you?

She let go of me and sat up, a look of mild surprise on her face.

You've never done anything like this before, have you? she said.

No.

She smiled. Good! Because neither have I, really—I mean, not with one of my own kind. She giggled. Not unless you count brothers as your own kind. Should we count brothers?

I don't know, I said. I don't know anything at all anymore. And I'm so ashamed. . . .

But why? she asked. Do you have brothers who played games with you too?

No, I said. But I don't *know* anything, don't you understand? We have to stop.

Not on your life, she said. She pressed against me, began rubbing her legs against mine. Play with me, she said.

But I can't.

Okay then, she said, and she grabbed me by the throat and began to squeeze. Now tell me to stop, she whispered. Tell me not to murder you, and what you'll do for me if I don't, and then you get on top of me and try to choke me. Come on. You're as hot as I am—I can tell. So try to throw me off or something.

I tried to pry Eva's hands loose from my neck, but this only made her begin squeezing one of my wrists so hard I nearly screamed.

We can play Houdini, she said, her eyes wild with expectation. That's when you get to hide inside my magic box and disappear.

She tried to force my hand under her skirt.

Hey, she said. You don't have to be scared. I can show you what to do.

She let go of my hand and then her hand was gliding along the inside of my thigh. I pressed my eyes shut, arched my back, and found myself thinking of the buckets of ice I used to carry in the summers for Ben, and how, when our arc lights became overloaded and the electrical plugging boxes and switches began sizzling, I would pack the boxes and switches with ice, listen to them hiss, and watch the steam rise.

Are you all right? Eva asked.

She was lying by my side.

I don't know, I said.

I think I got you so hot you passed out, she said.

Was I asleep? I asked.

I think so, but you looked so peaceful I didn't want to wake you. She kissed each of my eyes, and then she began to cry.

She covered her face with her hands, turned away from me.

What is it? I asked. Tell me—

No . . . I can't. . . .

Please.

But I never told anybody before. I never told anybody anything about what I've been telling you, and you're going to think ill of me, and our friendship will be ruined.

Why should I think ill of you?

Because of what I told you about me and my brothers. She turned to me again, her eyes pleading for forgiveness. I don't let them touch me anymore, she said. I carry a knife, see, and I'll use it too and they know it. I wounded one of them— George, he's the oldest—and nearly cut his McGregor off one time. But when I tried to stop them, they threatened to tell my father, and he would only have blamed *me* and smacked me around the way he likes to.

She was weeping more freely now and, without hesitating, I did what I wanted most of all to do but never knew I would do: I put my arms around her and pulled her close to me. It was easy. We were very quiet for such a long time that I thought she might have fallen asleep the way I had, but then I felt tears sliding along my cheeks, and I found that I was kissing her eyes the way she had been kissing mine, and that I was telling her I loved her.

I'm probably just a Dumb Dora, she said, snuggling close to me, but I've been frightened sometimes that I was going to live the rest of my life without ever getting married, or having children. At night sometimes, when I can't sleep, and whenever I'm at the Alhambra watching love scenes in moving pictures, I'm always imagining there's this man who's come to take care of me and love me, only he never has a face, and no matter how hard I try, I never see what he looks like.

I tried to imagine a story in which the man without a face was me, and I realized it had been a long time since I'd imagined a story taking place inside me. I touched Eva's cheek, and felt a surge of tenderness stronger than my mind's ability to make up stories, yet when I tried to pull Eva to me again, she pushed me away, and leaned on an elbow so that she could look at me.

Oh Joanna, she said then, given what we've been through—this is what I was thinking before you started getting me worked up again—why shouldn't we be able to just give and take some pleasure sometimes? I mean, who knows when a chance like this will ever come our way again?

I have to leave Milwaukee tonight, I said. I must be gone before morning, with the children, and please don't ask me why.

Then I'll go with you, Eva said.

I have to leave Milwaukee, I said, and I can't tell you why, and neither Eddie nor anybody else can know, or the children will be in danger.

But I can *help* you care for the children, Eva said. She sat up and took both my hands in hers. Listen. I can make believe I'm your cousin, or your sister. We can take the train down to Chicago, where nobody will ever find us, it's such a big city. Or we can switch trains in Chicago and change our names and the color of our hair and head west for Hollywood. You're so beautiful, you'd get to be a star in no time at all, and I could be a dancer—I'm a terrific dancer—or an usherette again if I had to, and we could take turns caring for the children, and I could help with everything, and we wouldn't be alone because we'd have one another, and just think of this too: we wouldn't ever have to worry about guys again either. . . .

But you'd be the star, I said, because you're more beautiful than I am. You're the most beautiful girl I've ever known. From the moment I first saw you, I thought so. I probably wanted to kiss you back then, even if you didn't know it— even if *I* didn't know it.

Then you're not angry with me?

Why would I be angry with you?

She touched my cheek with the back of her hand. I'd leave you alone whenever you ask me to, she said, and I wouldn't ever ask you why you had to leave Milwaukee, and I'd try not to bother you the way I bothered you before when you kept saying you didn't know anything.

It was true, I wanted to say. I didn't know if I was a man or a woman, or a boy or a girl, or a mother or a child, or dead or alive, or awake or dreaming, and when Eva smiled at me now I imagined myself walking right through her eyes, the way I might have done in a moving picture Ben and I were making, and into a meadow where new spring grass was the color of her eyes and her lips were the color of ripe plums. While I looped the film through the colored baths—film in whose frames Eva and I walked hand in hand and then lay down together in the grass and dissolved in one another's arms—I sensed that Ben was smiling at me, telling me that it was good not to lose the people you knew and loved.

But while I was imagining this, I was thinking too of how little I did know of all those people, like Eva and Ben and Gloria—of how little I knew of who they really were. I thought of how quiet Ben had always been, and it occurred to me that perhaps his true self had lived in silence the way the boy I once was lived inside the woman I'd become. I placed my hands on either side of Eva's face, and drew her to me—her mouth to mine—and, with as much tenderness as I possessed, kissed her.

When we separated from one another, her eyes were

moist and happy again, and I thought she was going to begin talking more about what her family was like, and asking me what mine had been like, but instead she suddenly shoved me down, leapt on top of me, pinned my wrists and straddled me, her knees pressed hard into my thighs.

Hey! I said. What are you doing?

Guess! she said, and added quickly, But not just yet, okay? Shhh . . . You're making me feel wonderfully drunk, and it's starting all over again—Holy Mother of Mary and Joseph, but it's starting all over again, only faster. Much faster. I'm dripping all over you—can you feel me yet? Oh dear God if we're not careful I may wind up drowning both of us.

She giggled, tilted her head back, opened her mouth as if she were howling, but without making any sound. She shuddered, then shuddered again, after which, as if somebody had whacked her across the back with a plank of wood, she suddenly fell down beside me.

Are you all right? I asked.

She said nothing. A second later she opened her eyes and smiled.

Never better, she said. She hummed to herself. Can you see me swimming? she asked. Oh my lord—I'm swimming across the ocean. I'm lost in the waves. I'm drunk and there's no creosote in the gin or ether in the beer and the only thing I'm thinking of is how to make *you* happy, because we certainly can't forget about you, can we? My greatest pleasure is still to come, see, because now, my sweetheart, I'm going to give *you* pleasure.

She put her hand under my skirt, on the inside of my thigh, and before I could tell my own hand to do what my body was telling it not to do, she had touched me where I wanted her to touch me most of all.

Oh my God! she said. Oh my dear sweet God, what have we here?

I turned my head to the side, put my fist into my mouth, and bit down.

I think we have more good news, ladies and gentlemen,

she said, even while she continued to caress me. That's what we have, I'm pleased to announce—more good news.

Then she flopped onto her back, but without letting go of me.

I can't believe it. I just can't believe it. Golly, Joanna—*Joanna?!*—you're a *guy!*

Yes.

All this time. All this time you've been a guy. No wonder. No *wonder!*

You're not angry with me?

Angry? she said. Oh my dearest darling, I can't believe it, and maybe we're both dreaming, but you've just made me the happiest woman in the world.

Then you didn't know? You couldn't tell?

Oh my dear sweet loving God in heaven!

You never suspected?

Oh Joanna, even if Joanna is not your true name—we can do anything we want, don't you see? We can be anything or anyone we want, in fact—brother and sister, husband and wife, sister and brother, sister and sister, brother and brother—I can be the guy and you can be the girl and then we can switch, and—oh my dear Lord—do you know what else—?

What?

We can play "Lollipop."

"Lollipop?"

She unbuttoned my blouse, ran her tongue down the center of my chest, nipped at my ribs, ducked her head under my skirt. And though I tried to imagine a moving picture inside my head the way I used to imagine stories for the moving pictures my family and I made, and though I tried to find a room inside me where I might store it, I found myself unable to imagine any stories or pictures, or find any room that might be capable of containing a remembered moment of what was now happening. And so, drifting away, I seemed to pass through time itself—through time without time—as if I were passing through a mirror without glass, or a mind without memory, or a man without a face, and when I returned to what seemed to be my ordinary senses, Eva was staring down at me the way she had in the infirmary and saying that if I told her the story of my life, she'd tell me the story of hers.

1927

While I sliced peaches into thin crescents, Regina dusted the kitchen table with flour, rolled out a second pie crust, and complained about Marvin: Where was he, and why was he always running away, and what if he didn't return home before it was time to leave? We wouldn't miss the matinee at the Granada, would we? Or the horse races at the county fair? Hadn't I promised we would see a moving picture of Lindbergh today, and that after the moving picture we'd go to the fair to see the races and the fireworks?

Regina talked on and on the way she did when we were alone, and I said that yes, I'd promised all those things. Today would be a day of surprises: the first surprise would take place at the theater, and Laura had promised that another surprise would be waiting for us at the fair.

The instant I spoke Laura's name, Regina turned her back to me.

Don't sulk, I said. Please? I stepped toward her, to take her in my arms.

You leave me alone, she said, backing away. And don't touch me. You're too hot and sticky.

Then stop your sulking.

What if I *like* to sulk?

If you do, your face will turn to stone, and when you grow up nobody will want to marry you.

Who cares? Nobody ever married *you*.

Sweat was pouring down my face—sliding into my eyes and mouth, running across my neck and shoulders and arms. My blouse and skirt were drenched, my thighs slick. Outside, though the sun had risen barely an hour before, the temperature, I was certain, had already passed one hundred degrees.

It was the morning of the Fourth of July—we had been living in San Bernardino, California, for nearly four months, in a single room of a one-story adobe house we shared with three Mexican families—and when I closed my eyes, I imagined Laura—that had been the name we chose for Eva when we left Milwaukee for Chicago—returning home, seeing the pies we'd baked, the sandwiches we'd made, the picnic basket I'd prepared.

Would she be happy to see me?

I grated nutmeg onto the peaches, poured in the currants and sliced apricots I'd been soaking in sugar water, squeezed on some lemon juice. I placed a block of hard, dark sugar in a cloth sack, pounded on the sack with a hammer, then spread the crumbled sugar onto the mixture. Regina criss-crossed narrow strips of dough on top of the pie, after which I brushed the strips of dough with melted butter, stuck in several cloves, and carried the pie to the oven.

When I opened the oven, drops of sweat fell onto the door and exploded in tiny bundles of steam. I set the pie on a rack, closed the door, looked out the window to the courtyard where children were chasing one another around the well. Beyond the well, in the shade of live oaks, a burro stood, immobile, dropping large turds onto what appeared to be a dead dog.

I thought of going outside and removing the dog before one of the children touched it, but as soon as the thought was there, the dog stood, limped off, and lay down again a few paces away. The dog was small and thin, its scabbed coat a dull silver in the morning sun.

Felipe and his father, Alvarez, were walking toward the well. Felipe was a tall, handsome boy of about twelve who often treated Marvin as if Marvin were his slave. Felipe caressed the dog's head, then lifted the dog high in the air, by its tail. The dog pawed at the air as if it were trying to swim. Alvarez held a hunting knife in his right hand and, with a single swift stroke, and without splashing blood upon himself, he slit the dog's throat.

A half-dozen children stood near Felipe, watching the dog's blood drip into the sand. To the side of our house, in the small stone and brick oven the Mexican women used for cooking, Alvarez's wife, Mara, lit a bundle of twigs, then fanned the flames with the hem of her skirt.

I looked for Marvin. He loved to play with the Mexican children, to hunt and fish with the boys, to let the girls dress him and fuss over him. Although I knew that Regina remembered me from the time when I had been a man, I did not think it ever occurred to Marvin to think of me as being anyone other than his mother.

As in other places, I thought, so it was here: nobody questioned who we were or where we had come from. Living for brief periods of time among people so poor that they themselves seemed, often, not to care if they lived or died, we were safe from whoever might still be searching for us.

I sat by the window and looked past grape arbors and fruit orchards that stretched all the way—perhaps three or four miles—to the San Bernardino foothills. Beyond the foothills, where the desert began, the peaks of the San Bernardino mountains, I knew, were still covered with snow, and I imagined lying in the snow and telling Laura what I often told her: that if we could just love one another again the way we had in the beginning, nothing else would matter—that we could survive *anything* that might happen to us.

Regina was wiping my forehead with a wet cloth.

Thank you, sweetheart, I said, and when I drew her hand to my lips, she did not pull away.

You're wet everywhere, Regina said. I've never seen anybody sweat the way you sweat.

In the courtyard, while Alvarez split wood with a hatchet, the children gathered around Felipe in a half-circle to watch him strip the skin from the dog. Once again, I was aware of a fierce pounding inside my head, like that of horse's hooves, and I found myself imagining the horses, and they were magnificent: handsome chestnut-colored stallions, lean ink-black fillies, a single custard-colored palomino. I saw a half-dozen horses racing along a dirt track at the fairgrounds, their necks and flanks white with lather, their bright, multi-colored silks brilliant in the mid-day sun, and while I watched them, I wrote out a title inside my head:

AT THE COUNTY FAIR

SAN BERNARDINO, CALIFORNIA
SEPTEMBER 22, 1927

Are you all right? Regina asked.

Yes, I said. And then, But the pies?

They're all right too, Regina said, and she laughed. Only you look so *dopey*, Mommy, like you're lost in another world!

Regina lifted the cloth from my forehead, dipped it in a bucket of water. I like it when we're alone, just the two of us, she said.

She pressed the wet cloth against my eyelids and began telling me about what was taking place in the courtyard, but in my mind I was still seeing the racetrack we would visit later in the day, though a swarm of flying insects with shimmering, translucent wings hung suspended, like a cloud, between me and the horses. There was a family lined up at the guard rail and I stared through the haze until it gave way and saw, no surprise, that the family was *my* family: Karl and Ben, Izzie and Flo, my mother and father—and they were all waving to me.

I let my gaze pass through the waves of heat that shimmered above the fire where Felipe was roasting the dog. I could see my mother's veil, white as snow, fluttering lightly in the air, and I heard myself explaining to her that I too, of necessity, when I had not had time to shave, had sometimes taken to wearing veils and to hiding my face.

They're home! Regina shouted. Look, Mommy—they're home! They're home!

I saw Laura coming toward us across the courtyard, dragging Marvin by the wrist. They reached the well, and Marvin broke away, ran to the other children, began chattering in Spanish. Laura let down a bucket, then drew it up, splashed water on her face, tilted her head back, and drank.

Felipe hoisted Marvin high above the other children, directly over the flames.

Mira! Mira! Mommy, Marvin called. *Mira! El perro . . . el perro viejo—! Viengo—!*

Felipe set Marvin on the ground, and Marvin ran toward me, a sack tight against his chest.

I stood by the door, my arms spread wide for him, but he rushed by me, scurried to the far corner of the room. The sack, I saw, was full of oranges.

She's drunk again, Regina said. She's *always* drunk.

Laura works hard, I said.

I put out my hand toward Laura, but she too walked by me.

Ha ha on you, Mommy, Regina said. Laura doesn't love you anymore.

The kid sure has a mouth on her, Laura said. Only the truth is it's too hot to love anybody, a day like this, even for money.

Hands on hips, Regina was chanting in sing-song: *Laura doesn't love you. . . . Laura doesn't love you. . . .*

I raised my hand, to strike her, but Laura stopped me. Leave the brat alone, she said, and get me something to drink.

Regina backed away, then curled up beside Marvin in the far corner of the room, where it was coolest, and where we stored our sacks of flour, rice, and beans. Marvin sucked on an orange and stared at me as if I were not there.

Oh Laura, I said. I'm just so sorry. . . .

You sure are, Laura said. You're one sorry soul, you ask me.

I turned to Regina, but she wouldn't look at me. I only wish things were different, I said. I only wish . . .

Who cares what you wish? Laura said, and she reached into the picnic basket, pulled out a peach, bit into it. God how I hate it here, she said. It's hotter than hell and not nearly as much fun.

You need to rest, I said. You need to let me bathe you and clean out your cuts.

I need a drink is what I need, she said. She put her face close to mine and breathed fumes of cheap whiskey on me. She pulled several dollar bills from her blouse, placed them in my hand, put a finger to her lips.

Listen, she whispered, I met this guy, see, so I have a plan—for how we can get the money to get out of here, you and me.

Then her jaw went slack, her eyes rolled up in their sockets, and she pitched forward into my arms. I carried her to our bed. Her left eye was swollen nearly shut, her hair matted flat to her skull. Her skin was cold.

Fetch some water, I said to Regina.

There were no hiding places in our room, but I couldn't see Marvin anywhere. Our mattresses lay upon the dirt floor at the western end, where the roof sloped down and the sun-dried walls were thickest. What clothes we had, including our uniforms and costumes, were stacked in orange crates between the beds. There were no closets, no crawl spaces—just four walls, one door, a window.

Regina returned with a bucket of water, and I began washing Laura's face.

Hey *senoritas*! Felipe called. I got something you like.

Felipe stood just outside our room, other children beside him. He made lewd sucking noises with his lips, jabbed a finger in and out of a circle he made with thumb and index finger.

Puta! Puta! he shouted.

The children took up the chant: *Puta! Puta! Puta!*

Regina touched Laura's forehead. She's burning up, Mommy.

Hey *puta*, Felipe said. My father don't even got to pay for it with you.

Listen, you Mexican moron, Laura said, sitting up. The best part of you ran down your father's leg, did you know that?

Felipe started toward us, but Marvin appeared in the doorway, a pearl-handled knife clutched in his fist. If Felipe moved even an inch forward, Marvin would, I knew, attack.

Felipe seemed to know it also, and he moved backwards.

My hero, Laura said softly.

I get you later, *gringo*, Felipe called. I get you good.

I dipped a cloth in water, began washing Laura's neck and shoulders.

Marvin *stole* the oranges, Regina said, and if old man Padilla catches him again, he said he'll come here one night and chop his hand off.

No he won't, I said. He just says that to scare you.

But he will—he *will*, Mommy. I know it.

Laura's cuts and bruises, I saw, were not so bad this time. Makeup would cover them. She was fast asleep now, her lower lip hanging down so that I could see its soft, pink underside. She was breathing heavily, rasping. Regina put her ear on Laura's chest.

It sounds terrible in there, Regina said.

Marvin stood in the doorway, a knife in one hand, an orange in the other.

She'll be better in a little while, I said. Take the pies from the oven, and then go outside and turn off the gas.

Will she still be able to dance this afternoon?

Yes.

Won't she fall down, from being so drunk and sick?

No.

Is she going to die?

Laura opened her good eye. Don't get your hopes up, kid, she said.

I washed Laura's face again, and thought of the time, two years before, when the four of us had stood on a rooftop in Chicago on the Fourth of July, watching fireworks bursting in the air above Lake Michigan, until a summer shower sent us back to our apartment. We read the children stories, put them to bed, and then returned to the roof, and became so lost in wetness and flesh—so easily generous with each other— that after a while we couldn't tell what was sweat, and what rain.

You need to rest, I said. Later—in a few weeks, when we've saved enough money, we'll go somewhere else. I promise. We'll find a quiet place by the ocean.

But that's the *plan*, Laura said. That's what I started to tell you about. This guy I met—Lex—the guy who's been wiring the theater for sound—the Vitaphone man? He can help us.

No, I said.

Why not?

I don't trust him.

Trust? Laura said. What's trust got to do with it? We don't need to *trust* him—we just need to *use* him so we can get some dough and get the hell out of here.

But what do we know about him? How do we know he doesn't want to turn us in for the reward?

How would he know who we are, the names we use and the way we look now? And how would anyone ever figure out why you left the same time I did? You're just being jealous again. She sighed. Believe me, I don't give anything to him I haven't given to you.

Laura began coughing. She gagged, heaved, then turned, snatched the cloth from my hands, covered her mouth.

The sweet fragrance of roasting flesh drifted into the room.

Look at the blood, Mommy, Regina said. Look—!

Laura lay back down. I want to die, she said.

I wiped blood from her mouth and chin.

Joanna?

Yes?

Keep me warm.

I lay down beside her.

I want to see the Pacific Ocean, she said. Will you promise me we'll see the Pacific Ocean?

Yes, I said. But don't talk now. Try to rest.

I think I liked you better before I knew you were a guy, she said. You think I don't remember the way things were with us in the beginning? All the things we dreamt of doing together? You think I *like* hauling ashes for all these stiffs?

I put a finger to her lips, and then, despite the foulness of her breath, I placed my lips where my finger had been.

It's funny, but I keep remembering names of places instead of men, Laura said. Don't you think that's funny?

Rest now, I said. Please. . . .

I'll say that for them—they got great names for places out here: Jackass Creek, Big Tooth, Ammonia, Rat Gulch, Sam's Lamb—that's my favorite, I think: Sam's Lamb, Oklahoma. Remember the theater we worked in there—the Oriental, with that old beat-up cyclorama we played merry-go-round on?

Shh.

Maybe what we can do when we get to the ocean is to get in touch with your Uncle Karl the way you said, and then change our names again so nobody can figure out who we are or were or . . .

She was shivering violently. I pulled her closer to me and she burrowed in against my neck, stuck her hands under my skirt. Her fingers were cold.

My chest hurts something god-awful, she said.

I talked to her about how, in the autumn, when we

reached the ocean, we would put the children into school, and how we would then have more time for each other—for walks along the beach, and picnics, and going to moving pictures together.

I motioned to Regina to fetch the jar of salve from under the sink—a mixture I'd made of goose fat, cloves, and a tincture of Mentholatum—and I rubbed the salve onto Laura's chest.

That feels good, Laura said. But listen to me, Joanna, okay? Let me tell you what we're going to do, see—what the plan is. What we're going to do is—get this—we're going to sell one of the kids, and then—

I must have cried out, for she pressed her hand against my mouth, and pulled me back to her.

I'm still cold, she said.

And you're talking crazy, I said.

But why should you care, she said. I mean, are they *your* kids?

She sputtered, sat up, and spat out an amazingly large quantity of blood and phlegm. I wiped her mouth and chin again, and while I did I searched through the rooms inside my mind until I found what I wanted: a picture of Izzie, rising in the river below the Palisades, a stream of blood going up before him, seeping from his mouth toward the water's surface. The blood was made of chocolate syrup and it spread through the water like a dark cloud, and when Izzie's head popped up out of the water and he licked his lips, waved to me triumphantly and began swimming to shore, I saw that I was waving back.

But the blood coming from Laura's mouth was real, I knew, and Izzie was dead, and we weren't living inside a story my family would turn into a moving picture.

I'll be fine, Laura said. And Lex has it all worked out—he's pulled this off lots of times before. Anyway, selling the kids isn't the real surprise.

I don't understand, I said.

You just make sure Marvin sticks close to us all day, she

said. Keep telling him about surprises, and about seeing Lindbergh, and leave the rest to me.

The Granada Theatre, despite its name, was modeled after a Viennese Opera House, with gorgeous rock-prism crystal chandeliers, velvet wallpaper, and, on the walls in gilt-edged frames, portraits of emperors, generals, and opera singers. It had recently installed a new refrigerating and ventilating system and Regina, Marvin, and I stood inside the lobby, cooling off with hundreds of others while we waited for the show to begin.

The theater's staircases were carpeted in thick wine-red paisley while elaborately curlicued gold and silver candelabras rose from the newel posts to light the way to the loge, the balconies, and the opera boxes. At the rear of the lobby, just past the Empress Josephine's Music Gallery where Mister Tarrantino played waltzes on a small Möller organ, and beside the marble bridal fountain where alabaster nymphs and cupids rose above small pools where real fish swam, there stood, in a zigzag arrangement, like an enormous Chinese screen, eight large display boards.

Upon these boards were affixed not only photographs of the stars featured in the current moving picture and stage show, but enlarged photos, newspaper articles, and architectural diagrams that charted the history of the Roxy Theater, which had opened in New York City five months before.

Regina and Marvin wanted to run off, so that, as always before shows, they could see who would be first to pick out Laura from among the dancers in the photographs. Before they could get away, however, the head usher, Hank Ross, a strapping young man who sometimes worked in rodeos and as a stunt man in moving picture Westerns, appeared before us, doffed his *kepi* in the air, and saluted the children. He handed each of them gold-tasseled programs, and said he had come to personally welcome them to a magical afternoon of magnificent entertainment.

Regina blushed while Marvin's brown eyes, nearly as dark as Gloria's, opened to twice their size. Hank offered to check my picnic basket and hat for me, after which, he said, he'd be pleased to escort the three of us to our seats. Or, in the time that remained before the show began, did we wish to see photographs of Lindbergh?

First we have to find Laura, Regina said, and she ran off, Marvin behind her.

Hank inclined his head toward me, remarked on how cool I looked on such a hot day, and then told me what a fine mother I must be to have such wonderful children. Might he have the privilege of accompanying the three of us on our trip to the county fair afterwards? He knew many of jockeys, barkers, and roustabouts, and could show us a terrific time. I thanked him, and explained that Laura would be joining us for the Fourth of July festivities at the fair—that she had promised us a surprise intended for our family alone.

Laura had been working at the Granada for five weeks as a dancer for Fanchon and Marco's Sunkist Girls. Although Fanchon and Marco had regular touring companies that went from city to city, we knew, from our time in Chicago, that some of their girls were always leaving—to get married, or to go into moving pictures, or because they became homesick or pregnant, and so Laura was usually able to hire on, as with other touring companies, as a fill-in.

She had become friendly not only with Hank, but with Mister Gollob, the Granada's general manager, and, as in other cities where we'd lived, she had persuaded them to give me—her older sister, she claimed, whose husband had died in France during the Great War, and who, with her help, was raising my two young children—part-time work as an usherette during those hours when Laura was not rehearsing or on stage.

In this way one of us was always able to be at home with the children, or, when this proved impossible, we were able to bring the children with us to the theater and leave them in the nursery.

Regina was tugging at my hand, telling me she'd found Laura, to come quick and see.

But where's Lindbergh? Marvin asked. You said I'd see Lindbergh.

Hank said that Lindbergh was getting his plane ready at that very moment—could Marvin hear the engine?—and that before long, right after the stage show, in fact, Lindbergh was going to make an appearance at the Granada.

I once saw a real airplane, Marvin said.

Hank told Marvin that most people in the world had never seen Lindbergh, and that, moreover, most of them had never seen a real airplane either. That's why today was such a great day, and when Lindbergh appeared, Marvin was going to feel as if he were right there in the plane with him.

I'm going to fly planes someday too, Marvin said. I'm not afraid.

Is that so? Hank said.

It's true, Regina said. He's not afraid of *anything*—that's why Mommy worries about him all the time.

After Hank left us, I pointed to a banner strung across the lobby's expanse, upon which banner was printed, in giant red, white, and blue lettering: THE STAGE COMES TO THE SCREEN.

Regina read the words aloud, and asked how a stage could be on the screen.

It's a magic trick, Marvin said.

Marvin's funny, Regina said.

No I'm not, he said. I'm just funny-looking.

Regina took my hand and led me through the crowd, to the display boards, where, under glass, in two large photographs—one where the Sunkist Girls were scantily clad dryads clinging to the limbs of tropical trees, and another in which, wearing drum majorette uniforms, they struck military poses as part of a stage-size American flag—they showed me which of the dancers was Laura.

Marvin asked if Hank was telling the truth about seeing Lindbergh, and I said yes—that Lindbergh's appearance was the first surprise I'd promised them. Regina and Marvin then led me to another board, so they could show me photographs of Lindbergh: Lindbergh at Roosevelt Field, Lindbergh taking off for Paris, Lindbergh arriving in Paris, Lindbergh riding through the streets of New York City with Mayor Walker. . . .

I left them, and moved to my left, where on two adjoining panels, under the heading THE CATHEDRAL OF THE MOTION PICTURE, there were photographs, drawings, and newspaper articles that told the story of the building of the Roxy Theater, from the razing of the car barn that had been on its site, to the digging of the foundation, the erection of the steel skeleton, and the gala opening night.

I thought of how entranced my father might have been had he been able to cross the river and watch the opening up of the ground, and the creation of underground chambers that provided for refrigeration, ventilation and humidification systems, a fire pump station and an ushers garrison, electric generators, lift mechanisms for stage and orchestra, dressing rooms, shower rooms, prop rooms, scene shops, upholsterers' shops, a carpenter's shop, and a menagerie in which camels, donkeys, and other animals would live while awaiting their time on stage.

He would also, I knew, have rejoiced in seeing all the numbers that were printed in large letters on the panels: that the Roxy seated more than 6,200 people for each of two daily performances; that it could accommodate 4,000 people in its lobby and rotunda; that it contained 60 bathrooms, 212 flush toilets, 45 shower stalls, 14 Steinway grand pianos, 7 organs, a musical library of more than 10,000 selections, and—on the topmost floor of the building, to the rear of the second balcony, where Mister Rothafel had his private offices, penthouse, bedrooms, dining facilities, and personal health club—the studio from which he sent forth his weekly radio broadcast.

Among all the photographs and charts, however, what fascinated me most of all was a small and precisely drawn floor plan that, as in an anatomical drawing, showed a cross-section of the theater and revealed its inner parts. How wonderful, I thought, that all of a person's needs, from birth to death, could be satisfied here—that one could make one's home here, as Roxy did, and never want for anything.

When, several minutes later, Mister Tarrantino sounded a fanfare of chords and segued into "Yankee Doodle"—and when the ushers came our way and announced that we should proceed at once to our seats for the show was about to begin, I found that I was still imagining that I was walking through the rooms of the Roxy—through tunnels and corridors, and up and down staircases and elevators, and that as I wandered from room to room, I was thinking, too, not only that one could, living in the Roxy, be entertained every day of one's life by the performances and moving pictures, but that, with the costumes, scenery, lights, and cameras available, one would, also, living there, have the wherewithal to transform one's dreams into stories, after which one could take the stories and store them safely in the theater's vaults so that they would never be lost.

I loved seeing the tiny lights on the musicians' stands, like fireflies, come on one by one, and I loved, too, the atmospheric prologues, the orchestral selections, and the performances that preceded the moving picture—the dancers, jugglers, acrobats, magicians, comedians, and the dog acts—but on this day, like the children, I was terribly impatient. So that when, at last, the final live act was ending—the orchestra playing "You're a Grand Old Flag" while the Sunkist Girls moved back and forth and up and down across the American flag, and colored spotlights and magic lanterns made it appear that fireworks were bursting all around them—and as various curtains came down, one after the other, starting from the rear of the stage—I felt my heart ease, and turned to the children.

Now, I said. And again: *Now!*

The Granada's house curtain was made of a material we called dream cloth—a sheer fabric interwoven with metallic threads that could catch the light in remarkable ways, and this curtain now fell in front of the others—the travelers—and after this the grand drapery, of satin and velvet, came down across the proscenium.

Below, the lights on the music stands went out one by one. When the curtains looped back to either side and opened again, revealing the enormous Magnascope screen, I breathed out. We were, thanks to Hank, seated in the front row of the loge, and from behind us, beneath the gilded catafalque that seemed to hold up the balcony—plaster noblemen on horseback—the projector sent forth its widening beam of light across hundreds of heads, and the usual announcement— LADIES PLEASE REMOVE YOUR HATS—appeared, after which the words MOVIETONE NEWS quivered for several moments and then, coming into focus, gave way, briefly, to a rectangle of undulating gray.

The audience applauded, but an instant later, when Colonel Lindbergh's face, in profile, appeared full on the screen, the applause ceased. Lindbergh was wearing an aviator's cap, and as he turned toward us and buckled its strap beneath his chin, the most extraordinary thing occurred: *We heard the sound of his airplane!*

Marvin rose from his seat, and had I not restrained him, he might have tumbled over the barrier in front of us to the seats below. Regina dug her nails into the palm of my hand.

Where? Where? Marvin cried out, and he whirled frantically, trying, I knew, to see if Lindbergh's plane had actually entered the theater.

Regina ducked her head, then looked up again. Some people were shouting and cheering, while others, like Marvin, were standing up and turning around, searching out the source of the sound. On the screen we watched Lindbergh climb into the plane. We saw him stow away provisions, saw the propellor spin, faster and faster, heard the stutterings of the plane's engine. The plane dragged its load along a runway, the roar of the engine grew louder still, and then, as the plane moved away from us, faded.

It's Lindbergh! It's Lindbergh! Marvin kept shouting. *He's here! He's here!*

On screen, a small crowd that had gathered around Lindbergh waved farewell to him, and, to our amazement, we could hear their voices join with ours, though our voices were dim against the rumbling of the plane's motor. The plane seemed to swim through mists, its right wing dipping toward the ground, and then—there was, in the theater, a vast collective intake of breath—the wheels left the ground. I held tightly to Marvin, and as the plane lifted off into the gray, fogged sky, we all, as one, were mute once more.

I had seen the same thing occur each time that I had, during the previous few days, been given a chance to work as an usherette: the silence lasted a full two or three seconds, and then the audience rose as one person and burst into exuberant applause and cheering—as much, I thought, for the miracle that had joined sound to picture as for Lindbergh.

Lindbergh! Lindbergh! Lindbergh! they shouted. *Lindbergh! Lindbergh! Lindbergh!*

The Movietone program itself lasted less than six minutes—there were more pictures of Lindbergh, and along with the pictures, titles that set forth facts most of us knew from radio broadcasts or newspaper accounts—after which there were two additional news features, each, again, with sound to accompany the images: a sequence in which a platoon of West Point Cadets marched to the music of a military band, and footage of the ruler of Italy, Mussolini, making a speech in Italian.

Once the news ended, the screen went to silver briefly, and then Ben Bernie appeared with his band, and smiled at us from the screen. "Good evening, ladies and gentlemen, or is this an afternoon performance?," he said, at which remark the audience exploded in laughter.

By the time we arrived at the fairgrounds, the fifth race of the day was about to begin, and Lex, holding a straw boater with one hand, and Laura's hand with the other, led us through the crowd to a roped-off area, close by the finish line, that he had reserved for us.

All the way from the theater, Lex had talked about money—about how much it cost to equip theaters with sound—ten thousand dollars was an average price—about how much commission he made on each installation, and about how he was grabbing in all he could before the craze for sound ended. He talked about the dozens of systems competing with one another—Vitaphone, Phonofilm, Photofilm, Syncrodisk, Vivaphone—and how some of the studios were planning to make features that, believe it or not, would contain *large* segments of spoken dialogue. He told us there were more than twenty-four thousand moving picture theaters in the United States, and that by the end of the year a full twenty thousand of them would have been wired for sound.

And what had made people ready for sound in theaters? he asked. Radio—that was the answer. Radio! Because nearly everyone in America now had sound in their homes. But it wasn't always like this. Did we know that at the beginning of the decade, fewer than fifty thousand homes in the United States had radios in them, and that nearly twenty million had them now?

As for himself, Lex said, he wasn't worried about whether sound did or didn't last because he had his own plans. The musicians and dance companies were worried plenty, though, for if you could put an orchestra and chorus on the screen and only had to pay for film rentals, why once your installation was paid for you'd never have to spend a plugged nickel for live entertainment again.

Some of the moving picture companies, in fact, were thinking about making *entire* feature films with sound, though nobody expected this to succeed. It would be like putting lipstick on the Venus DeMilo, Lex said, and this was the main reason why, as he'd been telling Laura, he was getting the hell out of the Vitaphone business.

The way I see it, he explained, is that I'm getting out of sound to go into something that's truly sound, if you catch my drift. He slipped his arm around my waist. What I want to do, see, is to get back into a line of work that doesn't have the unpredictable fluctuations in supply and demand that can kill an honest man.

I removed his hand from my waist. Laura sat in front of us on a wooden folding chair, our picnic basket beside her. Lex winked at me, rubbed his tiger's-eye ring against his jacket sleeve, then rested his hand on Marvin's shoulder.

Right, kiddo? he asked.

I saw Lindbergh, Marvin said.

You bet your sweet life—but not your sweetheart, right? Lex said. And added: The way I got it figured, people will always want to have children.

God only knows why, Laura said.

The sound of a bugle cut through the air. *The horses are on the track!* a man on a platform cried out through a megaphone—*The horses are on the track!*—and as soon as Marvin heard the man's words, he charged through the crowd, to the guard rail.

Regina hurried after Marvin. I'll watch him, she called. Don't worry, Mommy.

Quite the good little girl we have there, Lex said. And quite the good little girl we have here too, Lex said, while, under the pretense of bending over to show Laura the list of horses on his program, he let his free hand rest upon her thigh.

Outriders stood along the edge of the track on large Morgans and quarter horses to keep the racehorses from straying. The track was nearly a mile in circumference, its infield a vast oval of cracked earth and dead grass upon which there were several refreshment stands, a small hut for the placing of bets, and, close to the finish line, directly opposite us, a dozen or so large beach-style umbrellas that shielded people from the sun.

Marvin tried to slip under the railing so he could be nearer the horses, but Regina caught him and pulled him back. Beyond the finish line, by the paddocks, jockeys were carrying away their silks and saddles while young Mexican boys hosed down the horses. Rainbows shimmered in the spray. I started toward Regina and Marvin, but hesitated when I saw an elderly couple, dressed as if for an afternoon of boating on a lake—the man in a lemon-colored silk suit, and the woman in an elegant flamingo-pink dress whose hem grazed the ground—approach Marvin.

The man spoke to Marvin.

I felt my throat go dry. I looked across the track, as if hoping to find Ben there, filming the day's events, but I saw only his camera and his tripod, and they were lying on the ground. The camera had broken open, its compartments and gears exposed like a heart's chambers to the sun.

I looked back, at Laura, but she was fast asleep, her wide-brimmed organdy hat shadowing her face.

Eva—? I called, before I knew the word was on my tongue.

Laura did not stir and I turned away in time to hear the elderly man speak to Marvin. So tell me, my child, how are you enjoying the fair on this fine, summer afternoon? he asked.

I saw Lindbergh, Marvin replied.

The woman asked Marvin if he would like to cool off in the shade of her parasol.

I stepped in front of the woman, and took Marvin by the hand. We have to go now, I said.

But you *promised*, Marvin said, and he wrenched his hand free. You promised we would see the horse races and the fireworks and that there was going to be *another* surprise.

What a delightful child, the elderly man remarked. The man lifted his hat to me, revealing a bald head speckled with liver spots.

Come here, I said to Marvin. You come here now.

Marvin stuck his tongue out at me.

I pushed Regina aside to get to Marvin, but he was, as ever, too quick for me, and he moved away from me, along the railing.

You come here at once, I said again. Do you hear me?

Please, the woman said, her gloved hand upon my arm.

Though I have never been a mother, I believe I can understand some of what you must be experiencing. But be assured that—

Get away, I said. You get away from me, or I'll—

Or you'll what?

Lex stood beside me, grinning. He tipped his boater to the elderly couple while at the same time placing himself between us.

Ah ladies, ladies, he said. There is surely no cause for anyone to be more upset than is absolutely necessary. We are all civilized adults, are we not? And we have an arrangement.

Get away, I said to Lex. I'm warning you.

Lex took me by the arm, squeezed hard. Don't you be getting in the way of things now, goddamnit, he said through clenched teeth.

The woman's eyes were clouded with tears. My dear young woman, she said. I have heard your sad story, and I can only say that you have my assurance your son will be cared for with nothing less than all the love and kindness in our hearts. We are God-fearing Christians, and—

Shut your trap, I said.

Regina was pulling at my skirt. What about me? she said. What about *me*?

You shut up too, I said to Regina.

I watched a policeman, his eyes on us, make his way down from the grandstand.

As if I were not even there, the elderly man resumed his conversation with Marvin. Now let me ask you a question, young man, he said. Have you ever placed a wager on a horse race?

What's a wager? Marvin asked.

It's not something you put in your mouth on Sunday mornings, I'll tell you that, Lex said. What he means, kiddo, is have you ever made a bet?

No, Marvin said. But I saw Lindbergh.

The elderly man chuckled. Ah, he said. Then the boy, as

we who enjoy the sport of kings are wont to say, is, if you will forgive the expression—he bowed slightly to me—a virgin. Thus he will certainly bring us great luck today if he will be so good as to select a horse upon whom we will place a modest wager, yes?

Yes indeed, Lex said, and, turning to me and grasping my arm, he whispered the words "Little Bo Peep."

Little Bo Peep?

Leave them alone and they'll come home, wagging their tails behind them, he said. Got it? I've done this before. Afterwards, they'll never admit to having tried what they tried.

The woman spoke: Please tell us, then, Marvin—it is Marvin, isn't it?—which horse you think will win the race, and Mister Aldrich will take you with him to place the wager, and if the horse you choose should come in first, why you shall receive a handsome reward.

Marvin moved closer to me. Is *this* the surprise? he asked.

I looked past the track to where a long, low row of stables was located, and I wondered if we could, at night, hide out in one of them. I thought of bats, at dusk, flying out from the stables—swooping across the deserted track toward the brightly lit fairway.

So tell me, young man, Mister Aldrich asked, which horse do you choose?

That one! Marvin said, and he pointed to one of the outriders, a large dun-colored stallion.

Lex explained that we could not bet on that horse.

Why not? Marvin demanded. It's the biggest.

You must choose one of those with a number upon its saddle, Mister Aldrich said. Can you recognize numbers?

One two three four five six seven eight nine ten, Marvin said. He pressed his eyes shut. Ten nine eight seven six five four three two one.

Something soft, like a moth, fluttered at my ear. I reached up, to brush it away, and found myself touching damp skin. I turned. Laura's lips were at my ear. Everything will be fine, she said. Just do what Lex says, and don't be stupid, okay? Like I've been telling you, this is our chance.

And may I present the boy's Aunt Laura, Lex said. Laura, this is Mister and Mrs. Aldrich, of whom I have spoken.

Laura curtsied, then covered her mouth with her hand and started coughing again.

Number five, Marvin said. I choose number five.

An excellent choice, Mister Aldrich said. He looked at his program: Portland's Pride, a two-year-old filly, at seven-to-one.

Mrs. Aldrich turned her sad eyes on us once more. We are forever in your debt, she said.

You don't have to be, Laura said.

Excuse me? Mrs. Aldrich said.

You have something for me, right? Laura said. You're going to give me something so that you won't be in our debt.

Is it true then? Mrs. Aldrich asked, a gloved hand upon her bosom. She turned toward her husband. Is this really happening?

I hope to God it is, Laura said.

Lex had opened a folding chair, and he helped Mrs. Aldrich seat herself upon it.

And may I take that from you for a moment? he asked, gesturing to the knitting bag she carried over her arm, a bag from which three knitting needles, their blunt ends upwards, extended.

Mister Aldrich and Marvin were already walking toward the betting booths that were situated below the grandstand.

Lex gave the knitting bag to Laura.

Marvin! I called, and started after him. Stay where you are! Do you hear me?

Lex stood in my path. Let the boy enjoy himself, he said.

The policeman, standing behind the rope that contained our section, tipped his cap to Mister Aldrich as Mister Aldrich and Marvin passed him. Did he know? Had Lex paid him so that he would detain us while Lex took off on his own?

Lex reached inside his jacket and withdrew an envelope that had been sealed with an embossed circle of golden wax. He handed the envelope to Mrs. Aldrich, said he would fetch her more lemonade and, if she wished, some smelling salts—the heat was brutal today, was it not?—and he assured her that all was in order: that the envelope contained everything she and her husband would need should any authority ever question the legitimacy of the transaction.

I snatched one of the knitting needles.

The policeman seized my arm and asked me what I thought I was doing. I lashed out, saw a thin ribbon of red curl from his cheek.

You! I called out. *You!*

Marvin stopped. I swiped at Mister Aldrich with a knitting needle, and he covered his eyes and fell backwards.

The policeman tried to grab my arm, but I struck out at him again.

The horses are approaching the starting gate! the man with the megaphone cried. *The horses are approaching the starting gate! All wagers down! All wagers down! Ladies and gentlemen, the horses are now approaching the starting gate. . . .*

The policeman blew on a whistle. Marvin had returned, and was kicking furiously at the policeman's shins. *Chinga tu madre!* he shouted. You let my Mommy go! You let my Mommy go! *Chinga tu madre . . . !*

People were crowding around us, blocking out the sun. Lex was asking people to move back, telling them to get help, to call for a doctor. Then he pointed to the policeman.

That officer is molesting this innocent young woman and her son! he said. Shame! Shame!

Laura was at my side. Hurray for Marvin, she whispered.

Lex tried to grab the knitting bag from Laura, but she pulled it to her chest. Oh no, sweetie, she said. This is mine—all mine.

The policeman withdrew a nightstick, but Marvin saw it and jumped on the policeman's arm.

Mister Aldrich was standing at the front rim of the crowd, blood streaming down his cheek. Would you kindly return my wife's knitting bag? he said.

Not on your life, Laura said.

I pointed at him. That man tried to kidnap my child! I declared. He tried to kidnap my son!

Don't overdo it, okay? Lex said. Let's just get the hell out of here.

Marvin was pounding on the policeman's nose with both fists and when the policeman let go of me, to ward off Marvin, I did what Izzie had long ago taught me was the one certain way, in any fight, to gain the advantage: I kicked the policeman where he lived, between his legs.

The policeman moaned, dropped his nightstick. His face was a balloon of mud and blood.

Marvin picked up the nightstick, lifted the policeman's hat, whacked him on top of his head with the nightstick, then replaced the hat. I saw other policemen surrounding Lex, grabbing him.

Laura took my hand. Come on, she said. She set our picnic basket down at the policeman's feet.

We ran through the crowd and we didn't stop until we had passed the betting windows and arrived at the far side of the grandstand.

This way, Laura said, and we followed her through a passageway, down three steps, and into a tube-like tunnel where we had to brace ourselves against the sides to remain upright. We raced ahead, the children delighted to hear their voices echo against the ribbed metal—"Hurray! Hurray!"—while, between fits of coughing, Laura informed me that when we arrived at the other end the surprise she had promised would be waiting for me.

I heard the sound of a single gunshot.

The tunnel rose and we made our way back into sunlight

and found that we had passed beneath the racetrack and were on its far side, in front of the stables. The race had already begun—thus the gunshot—and where the horses, in a clump, were moving around the track, I saw a cloud of silk and dust.

There she is, Laura said.

I looked to where Laura pointed and saw a stable boy sitting on an overturned pail, whittling at a stick. The boy stood, tossed away the stick, took off his jockey cap, and smiled at me.

Gloria! I cried. Oh my dear Lord! Gloria . . . !

I knew her at once, despite the years, and I ran to her and we fell upon one another, and kissed one another's faces everywhere.

Although the lines in her face, and the dullness of her eyes—more gray than brown—showed that the years had been cruel to her, I would have known her anywhere. I wanted to ask her a thousand questions, to tell her a million things—but all I could do was laugh and cry and cover her with kisses and hold to her, until—had two seconds passed? two minutes?—Laura told me we should cut out the smooching, that we had to hurry, that she would explain everything—how Gloria had escaped from prison, and how she'd figured out our trail, and how she'd met up with Lex, and how the three of them had devised a scheme whereby we could still get that ten thousand dollar reward we'd left behind at the Alhambra—but there was no time now, and if there was one thing she was determined to do, it was to put her bare tootsies in the waters of the Pacific before the sun rose.

You're taller, Gloria said.

Yes, I said.

I mean, you're taller than me now.

Marvin tugged at my dress, and I realized that he and Regina were standing beside me.

Gloria seemed to see them for the first time.

Oh my God! she exclaimed. Oh my dear sweet Jesus. I never thought. I never imagined. . . .

The children's hands in mine, I spoke, This is your mother, I said.

You're our mother, Regina said to me. You're *lying* to us again.

I'll explain, I began.

There's no time, Laura said.

Gloria came near, bent down.

Marco? she said.

My name isn't Marco, Marvin said, and he held to my skirt and hid behind me.

Listen: there's no time, Laura said again. They'll be coming after us—

She's your *real* mother, I said again, though I realized, even as I spoke, that my words could make no sense to them.

You're my Mommy! Marvin cried out, and he let go of my skirt. *You're* my Mommy!

I reached out to him. Come here, I said. Please. . . .

You'll never catch me, Marvin said. Never never never never!

Marvin ran off, toward the track.

Gloria looked at each of the children, then at me.

You did a good job, she said. You've been a good mother, Joey.

Laura opened the knitting bag. Holy shit, she exclaimed. She brought the bag to me, so that I could see, at its bottom, where skeins of wool should have been, thick bundles of money. You want this—or you want them—you choose, okay? Laura said. But I'm getting my ass out of here. She looked inside the bag again. Oh sweet Mary mother of Jesus. . . .

Marvin! I called. You come back here at once.

He won't listen to you, Regina said. She looked at Gloria. He never does what *anybody* tells him to, not even Mommy.

I started after Marvin, but when he saw me coming, he ducked under the railing and ran onto the track.

You come back here at once, I said.

I glanced to the left, where the horses were rounding the near turn for their second time around the course.

Marvin! I called. The horses! The horses! Come back *now*!

Marvin stuck out his tongue at me. *You're my Mommy*! he shouted. Say it. Say that you're my real Mommy and she's not!

All right, I shouted, but I was not sure he could hear me against the roaring of the horses' hooves. *All right—I'm your Mommy. Yes. I'm your Mommy, all right? I'm your Mommy. . . .*

Marvin lifted a hand, waved, and started walking back toward me.

Gloria gasped. Oh my God, she whispered. Oh my dear sweet Jesus—!

Regina shrieked.

The horses flew across the space where Marvin had been, and then they were gone, racing for the far turn and the homestretch.

Holy shit, Laura said, softly.

I was on the track. I lifted Marvin's body in my arms, told him to talk to me. I heard Laura tell me there was no time. I heard the crowd cheering, and then I heard Gloria say the name Angelina. Had the horses and riders even noticed that Marvin was in front of them? I set Marvin back down on the ground, watched blood trickle through his hair into churned-up clods of earth.

Leave him, Gloria said.

What?

Come on, she said, taking my hand. If we don't get out of here now, they'll get *all* of us.

People were moving toward us, across the track's infield. I looked around. Where was Laura?

Come on, Gloria said. Didn't I used to tell you it was bad luck to have only one kid—that it was best, since you never knew what could go wrong in this life, to always keep a spare?

Marvin's blood continued to leak onto the track, pooling

there, and I imagined that were I high up in the sky looking down at him—were I filming the moment—his hair and his blood, in a close-up, might look like flood water spreading through freshly plowed land.

But how, I wondered, could I be imagining such images at such a time?

Listen, Joey, Gloria said. We don't have time for grief now, you know what I mean? Come on.

She put an arm around me and I let her lead me away, back toward the stables. Her grip was strong. I wondered what her life in prison had been like, and I tried, for an instant, to calculate how many months, days, hours, and minutes had passed in the more than six years since we had last seen each other. I put my arm around her waist.

Angelina was crying, and when I put my hand out to her, she took it.

Take your Mommy's hand too, I said.

1930

Karl was waiting for me on the patio, studying the week's Torah portion as he did each Saturday morning before we left for synagogue, but before I could join him, Eduardo, who was in charge of the house servants, detained me with a gloved hand and told me that Mrs. Davidoff—Karl's wife—wished to see me privately in her quarters.

I followed Eduardo through the dining room and past the main kitchen—quiet, as always, on the Sabbath—and along the breezeway that looked out upon the swimming pool and tennis courts. Eduardo talked to me of how much he admired Karl for his devotion to the Sabbath, and of how much more he admired Lady Eleanora for her devotion to Karl.

It was an especially clear and gorgeous early summer day, yet the air was unseasonably cool. In my mind I was floating down the Hudson River in a sailboat, Izzie suspended from a parachute in the sky above, the parachute undulating in the air currents like a pale sea anemone. I imagined Ben watching us from the cliffs of the Palisades, and I reminded myself that inside his camera, to fix Izzie and myself there forever, the shutter created brief periods of light that alternated with long periods of darkness. Later on, when we watched our shadows move upon a screen, the process would be reversed: within the projector, long periods of light would alternate with brief periods of darkness. I saw myself drifting under the enormous span of steel and concrete that would soon, I knew, become the world's longest suspension bridge, linking New York City to New Jersey.

Eduardo was talking to me, but I hardly heard his words. I apologized to him for being distracted.

Ah, Master Joseph, he said. You are a dreamer, aren't you?

Yes, I said, smiling. Joseph the cockeyed dreamer, that's me.

I followed Eduardo through the rose garden, then past fields of summer melons, their leaves glossy and dew-drenched in the morning air. I inhaled the aroma of fragrant pepper trees, looked beyond vineyards and fruit orchards to the low-lying western hills that shielded us from the Santa Ana winds.

Lady Eleanora is looking especially radiant this morning, Eduardo offered.

She is a beautiful woman, I said.

The most beautiful woman in the world, if I may say so, for the beauty of God's loving spirit shines forth from her eyes.

Yes. You're kind to say so, Eduardo. And how is your family?

Ah! Eduardo exclaimed and he began talking about his family with enthusiasm, and of how he had, the night before, lit a candle to the Virgin Mary in gratitude for all that Karl had done for them.

Your uncle does great good in the world, Eduardo said.

Karl had, in fact, obtained work for virtually all of Eduardo's relatives, and that evening, when the sun set and the Sabbath ended, Eduardo would make use of Karl's private theater to show his family the moving pictures of Pancho Villa that Karl had purchased—moving pictures that contained sequences in which Eduardo could be seen alongside Villa.

And one day soon, Master Joseph, I hope you too, like your uncle, and like my sons, will find a wife worthy of you.

Had I seen the film, Eduardo wanted to know.

Yes, I said. You were quite the dashing young man, Eduardo.

I was very foolish, Eduardo said. But I was happy.

In 1914, I had learned from Karl, Pancho Villa sold the motion picture rights of his war to the Mutual Film Corporation. Villa had contracted to fight his battles by daylight, had delayed attacks on specified cities until Mutual could arrive with its film-making crews, and had staged executions and skirmishes expressly for the cameras. D. W. Griffith was hired to make a moving picture from the footage, but the footage had, in the years since, vanished, melted down, some said, for their silver nitrate content.

Eduardo, while attending to Karl during the production of *King Solomon and the Queen of Sheba*, had shown Karl photographs of himself and Villa, and had led Karl to an orphanage in Zaragoza, run by Franciscans, where Villa, on his way to Juarez after the murder of President Madero, had deposited the reels of film.

With the money they received from Karl for the reels of film, the Franciscans had rebuilt the orphanage in Zaragoza, and they were now completing the construction of a new orphanage in Los Angeles. Later in the day, between the morning and afternoon prayers, Karl and I would visit the orphanage, and the Franciscans would bestow their blessings upon us.

Eduardo and I passed the carriage house and the stables. Beyond them, to the east, workers were already in the fields, hosing down the vegetable and flower gardens. We turned away, walked across a tiled courtyard, then along a cloistered passageway that connected the main building to Karl's private quarters.

I had been living with Karl for three years now, and it

still surprised me that he had become the kind and generous man he was. It was as if, I sometimes thought, Ben's spirit, upon his death seventeen months before, when our building in Fort Lee had burned down, had made its way into Karl's soul.

Karl had been married to the woman known to the world as Lady Eleanora for all but four months of these three years, and he claimed that the transformation in his character had been brought about because of the love they had found with one another.

Lady Eleanora opened her door and we embraced. I moved away from her at once, heard a door close behind me.

Ah Joey, Gloria said, taking me by the hand. There's nothing to worry about with Eduardo. Come and sit with me for a few minutes. I got something important to tell you. Angelina's gone out for her morning ride—she loves that horse like it's Valentino reborn, yeah?—so you don't have to worry about her coming back soon. So come and sit with me. I have news.

I sat beside Gloria on her bed, and she placed my hand, palm down, upon the soft flesh of her stomach. She was wearing a sheer peach-colored negligee, and I could feel the heat of her body rise through the silk.

I haven't told anybody yet, not even Karl, she said. I wanted you to be the first.

I pulled away but she took both my hands with her own. No, she said. Please? Just listen to me a minute. This way maybe Angelina can have a brother again, don't you see?

I said nothing, but Gloria kept talking, telling me to listen to her, telling me of the unexpected ways in which she found herself happy these days, and while she talked I saw myself, like young David, fleeing through the forest from King Saul, and I found myself rehearsing lines I would speak the next day—"Who is that uncircumcised Philistine that he dares defy the ranks of the living God?"—when we resumed work and I would be playing the roles of both David and Jonathan.

This is good news, Joey, believe me, and it won't change nothing between us, Gloria said. Karl's gonna be thrilled when he hears, but I didn't want you to be surprised if you were there when I told him.

Is it his child or mine?

What kind of idiot question is that—his or yours? she asked. Jesus! It's *mine*, goddamnit.

Gloria walked to the far end of her room, pushed open the shutters, stepped outside onto her balcony.

Only I'll tell you this, buster, she said, turning and facing me. As much as Karl worships us both and is gonna love the brat when it's here like he never loved nothing else in his life, if he ever finds out about you and me, he'll kill the two of us without counting to three. He's like Vito that way.

Gloria lit a cigarette, inhaled, and I imagined myself tumbling through clouds of smoke as if I were Tom Thumb— past her lips and teeth, down her throat and into the warm hollow of her body. I missed being a woman, I wanted to tell her. Could she understand that? I missed being called mother by the children. I missed brushing Angelina's hair, and having her brush mine. I missed tending to the children's needs— bathing them, cooking for them, shopping for them, cleaning up after them, making their beds, breaking up their fights—I missed all those ordinary chores that had made up the infinite complexity of any hour or day of our lives. And I missed, too, the times I would find a quiet place in a strange city—a bench in a park, the grassy bank of a pond, a school playground— where I could sit with other mothers and watch our children at play.

I missed sharing stories with other mothers about how they dealt with their children's colds and tantrums. I missed asking them questions about what to do when one of the children had a rash, or refused to eat, or had trouble falling asleep. I missed being told what a charming devil Marco was, and that Angelina would be as pretty as I was when she grew up. I missed exchanging recipes, and talking about where to shop for the best clothing bargains, and how to let down dresses and trousers so the hemlines wouldn't show. I missed having other mothers dote on me when I would show them tricks for putting on makeup, and I missed, most of all, times when we could stay in a city for more than a few weeks and a mother came to trust me enough to talk with me about her hopes and her dreams—of what her childhood had been like, of why and how she had or had not married a man she truly loved, and of what she would give to be rid, if only for a day, of her child or children or husband so that she might start life all over again.

We talked with one another about what to do when two or more children needed your attention at the same time, and about ways to get children to go to sleep. We talked about wishing we were wealthy and living in elegant mansions with dozens of servants, and we talked about wishing we had husbands who were kind and tender to us.

I stayed where I was, Gloria backlit on her balcony by the morning sun, and I wondered if anything I desired or loved would ever again be mine.

If Karl catches you smoking on the Sabbath, I said, he'll be furious.

Karl?! Gloria exclaimed, and she threw down her cigarette, ground it out with her heel. Karl's a goddamned hypocrite. The Sabbath my ass—him riding around in his car all day like he didn't arrange the whole thing—like he thinks he can fool God.

Gloria glared at me, and when she did, her rage made her more beautiful and desirable than ever. She made fun of how, seated in his touring car, Karl would soon be talking to his chauffeur as he did every Saturday: "Now if someone were to see to it that I arrived in a place where I could pray with ten Jewish men, he would not be sorry. And if someone were to see to it that I might visit my orphans . . ."

But what was mine? I wanted to ask Are *you* still mine? I was afraid, though, that if I let my thoughts become words, Gloria would think me childish. I went to the balcony, and saw Angelina emerge from the woods on the other side of the pond that lay below us. Angelina, I realized, was the age I was on the day the Leskos' horse fell through the ice, and before long she would be the age I was when I first met Gloria, and soon Gloria would be the age my mother was on the day my father fell down the elevator shaft.

How could it be?

I tried to imagine that I was watching Gloria fall asleep. I saw myself placing a small black doctor's bag upon her night table, and opening it so that, while she slept, I could transform her into the young woman she had once been. I saw her sitting on a chair, her neck exposed, her blond hair draped backwards into a sink. I was beside her, warm water flowing through my fingers while I rinsed the dyes from her hair.

I drew a knife from my doctor's bag, tested its edge. I had not been in the room when the surgeon Karl hired had transformed Gloria into Lady Eleanora—when the doctor had straightened the bone in her nose, and dimpled her chin, and stitched in the tiny beauty mark beside her mouth—but in my mind I was carving away pieces of flesh and bone from her face until little of her remained—until, in my mind. I was seeing words on a screen:

JOEY AND GLORIA

REUNITED AT LAST!
HOLLYWOOD JUNE 17, 1930

Gloria was touching my face, telling me I was the only man she had ever truly loved or ever would love. When she touched me it was as if she were touching her own body, she said. I was her second skin—her second self!—did I know that? She talked again about her friend Melissa, who had died in the electric chair for having murdered her husband—she had shot him dead, three bullets to the chest—and of how she had spent Melissa's last night on earth in Melissa's jail cell, the two of them holding to one another until dawn.

Was the child mine or Karl's? she repeated, then laughed.

So if it looks like you or if it looks like him, it'll look like either of you or both of you, right? Hey—your uncle's a good man, Joey. I didn't mean to make fun of him before. He never hurts me.

Do I look like him?

More than you looked like your father.

Really?

Really.

Does that mean you think my mother and . . . ?

No, sweetheart, she laughed. I was just teasing.

Nobody knows what happened to my father, I said. When our building burned down he wasn't in it, and sometimes I like to imagine he's been wandering across the country with his musical instruments, following the same route I took with your children, and that one day soon he'll show up here, and Karl will take him in, and then . . .

Ah, you're wonderful, Joey, you and all the cockeyed stories you got inside that head of yours.

But what *good* are they? I asked.

Listen, she said. Your stories kept me alive once upon a time. Like I told you, it's what I did all those years when things got bad—like somebody would be beating the crap out of me, or men would be let in at night to do things to me you don't want to know about. And while whatever was happening was happening I'd do like I remembered you telling me you did: I'd pretend there were rooms inside my head and that I was living in *them,* and that I had a different life in those rooms than the one I was living in.

But you and Karl . . . ?

Hey—I don't love Karl the way I love you, she said. And I don't love you the way I love Angelina. And I don't love Angelina the way I loved Marco. And I didn't love Marco the way I loved Melissa. And I didn't love Melissa the way I loved Vito. Hey—I've got enough love for everybody, Joey. I got enough to go round for a while, believe me.

I imagined my father arriving at Karl's estate, and knocking on the front door, telling Eduardo who he was, and I wondered if it would be possible to draw a map of my father's brain that would have shown you where things had changed—where bridges had blown up and rivers had gone dry or flooded over, where cities had been burned to the ground and forests and fields had been ravaged—and I wondered too at what points on the map of his mind, as with subway lines in New York City, you could switch over—where you could transfer thoughts, feelings, pictures, and memories from one set of tracks to another.

What does it mean, anyway, to *want* me? Gloria asked. What am I—a cup of coffee or an automobile? All you want is what men always want. All you really want is to have me for yourself.

Maybe.

Maybe my ass. But you know what? Life doesn't have to be like that. You and me, I think we have something better than that, don't you see?

No.

Friendship, Joey. It's the big thing, take it from me. Friendship—between a man and a woman, or a woman and a woman, or a man and a man—it's something that lasts through whatever ups and downs come along and without everybody working their asses off to *get* things or to *prove* things, you know what I mean?

No.

Because you don't want to. Listen: you name me one great love story between a man and a woman that ends happy. Name me just one. Come on—

I thought of David and Jonathan, and then of Gloria and Melissa, and I thought of saying that sometimes friendship could end the same way love did.

We'll be fine, you and me, no matter what, Gloria said. So don't be such a jerk. What should we do—tell Karl the truth and get us both killed? Like my old man used to say, what good's truth if it don't put food on the table? And anyway, it's not like Karl's gonna live forever.

There was a knock on the door.

That must be Eduardo, Gloria said. So you go and take care of yourself, yeah? Karl's waiting to go pray with you, but don't say nothing to him until after I break the news. Promise?

Gloria's fingers were on the back of my head, and they seemed to slip under my scalp, tracing the shape of my skull, sliding along bone, searching for openings.

Trust me, Joey, she said. Trust me, okay? I got a plan for us.

Lex had a plan too, I said.

Lex was a jackass.

I imagined Gloria's fingers moving inside my head, going from room to room, putting out lights one by one and closing doors.

Trust me, she said again, and then she kissed me. Trust me now, when you're not the boy you once were and I'm surely not the girl. Trust me now, Joey, because if you do, see, *all* our dreams can still come true.

After we passed through the studio gates, we drove for about a half hour to where the desert began and to where, the day before, we had filmed a battle scene. We stood at the top of an enormous sand dune upon which a wooden platform had been erected. Below, the desert was the color of honey and apricots.

On the day the Temple was destroyed, Karl said, the Messiah was born. I like that, what the rabbi spoke about today—he told me something I didn't know, you see, but what I still don't understand is why, when Saul spared goats and cattle in a conquered city, to use for sacrifices to God, God was displeased.

Below us, hundreds of people, Mexicans and Chinese for the most part, were carving up dead horses and cattle—killed during the battle scene we had shot the day before—and were carrying away slabs of meat, for food. When they realized that Karl had arrived, they stopped their work. Karl waved to the people below—they cheered—after which we sat in chairs Karl's assistants brought for us. Then Karl made a fluttering gesture with the back of his hand, a sign to the people below that they should resume their work.

He joked about the fact that God, who had an even worse production schedule than he did, he said, took a day off after he worked six. And think of this, he continued. Bathsheba bore David a son, but God caused the son to die. Was God jealous, do you think?

Maybe, I said.

Karl roughed my hair, put his mouth close to my ear. I mean, think of it, Joey—all the women David was screwing, and all the children he was begetting, but when it came to the one woman he truly loved, God made sure that from her he got nothing. Oh, our God was a very jealous and angry God back then, especially when it came to those he chose to put in high places. Which says to me that you and me, as fortunate as we've been so far, we still have to be careful. Do you understand me?

Maybe.

When David conquered cities that God or the Prophet Samuel told him to conquer, Karl said, he slaughtered everything he found: men, women, children, animals. He cut off the hands and feet of soldiers. He burned women and children to death. He chopped off the heads of those who defied him and had the heads displayed throughout his kingdom. He took other men's wives for his own. He danced without clothes in front of his armies, and bragged of all the children he'd fathered.

Karl put his arm around me, kissed my cheek, tugged on my ear.

That's why you should agree with me about having to be careful—about not being foolish, Karl said. Only listen—when you look at what's going on down there, what does it remind you of?

The lake, I answered.

Karl nodded. But doesn't it seem to you a small miracle, he said, that the lake has become a desert, and New Jersey is California, and you and me, we're together in the Promised Land where we have three hundred and fifty days of sunshine a year for making our moving pictures . . . ?

We sat in silence for a while, watching the people below chopping at animals with axes and knives, carrying off the heads of goats and horses. Then Karl began talking about the good fortune God had bestowed on us, and while he did, lines of Chinese and Mexican men, women, and children, meat stacked upon their shoulders and backs, walked slowly toward us, up the hillside.

When the men, women, and children reached the top of the hill, they made two lines, passing to either side of us, the men stopping and bowing their heads to Karl, and when they did, Karl raised his hands above them and recited the priestly blessing in Hebrew, asking that the Lord bless the Chinese and Mexican families and keep them, and cause his countenance to shine upon them, and grant them peace.

I'll tell you this, though, Karl said. If I didn't have you and Gloria with me—if we didn't love one another and weren't loyal to one another the way we are—all of this—this little empire I've made—would mean nothing to me.

Then Karl seized my chin in his hand, forcing me to face him. His eyes were on fire, and his face came so close to mine I thought he was going to kiss me, but suddenly he let go, sat back, and laughed.

Ah, you're a good boy, Joey, he said. You've been a great blessing to me in my old age, the way Benjamin was to Jacob. That we should be together now when everybody else, one way or the other, is gone—that you and Gloria found one another, and that I married her, and that Angelina has become my daughter, and that soon she'll have a brother or sister— it's all a miracle and a mystery, which is why I'm beginning to think I understand what it means to say that on the day the Temple was destroyed the Messiah was born. What I think it means is that the best can be born from the worst—that good can come from bad, and sweetness from things rotten and diseased—but only, and this is crucial, only if you don't ever, ever forget what it is that you lost.

Between the morning and afternoon services Karl and I paid brief visits to two orphanages—the Franciscan orphanage and the Simon Levine Home for Jewish Boys—as well as to the Hannah Levine Home for the Aged, the Isaac Davidoff Home for the Blind, the Marco Antonelli Home for Unwed Mothers, and the Eva Bornstein Home for Chronic Diseases. All these institutions had been built with and were being maintained in large part by contributions from Karl. Karl had saved our visit to the Ben Davidoff Home for the Deaf for last—for when our evening prayers were done—because, he said, there was something there he wanted me to see that could not be seen until the Sabbath ended.

When we arrived, my mother was waiting for us in the home's lounge, asleep in her wheelchair. Mister Von Stroheim stood next to her, in a tight-fitting officer's uniform, fingering his monocle. As soon as he saw us, he snapped to attention.

Von Stroheim, he stated.

I bent over, kissed my mother on the forehead.

Her eyes, above her veil, opened.

Ah Joey, my Joey, she said. I knew you'd come and save me.

Karl pointed to the front of the sitting area where a small moving picture screen, perhaps six feet wide and four feet tall, had been set up. Then he took my mother's hands in his, asked her about her health, about how the trip went, getting from the Home for the Aged to the Home for the Deaf.

Oh, it's a very long way to go, from there to here, my mother said. I'll tell you that. And for what? To be disappointed again? But that's the way it is, even when you get old and lose important things, like your nose and your husband.

Well, Karl said, if I'd had your life, I'd be bitter too.

Bitter? Who's bitter? I'm disappointed is what I said. What are you, deaf or something?

My mother laughed, then stopped abruptly, reached up and ran a finger along the scar in Mister Von Stroheim's face.

So tell me something, my friend—could you still go for a girl like me?

Mister Von Stroheim lifted my mother's gloved hand, kissed the air between his lips and her fingers. You are an exceptionally beautiful woman, Hannah. I have admired you from the moment I first had the privilege of seeing your face upon the silver screen. That is why I intend to do my utmost to induce you to play a role in a motion picture I am hoping soon to complete.

Talk to me, my mother said. Let my brother hear.

There is a scene in this film, you see, of which I am most fond, where, upon the tip of his sword, our hero lifts a pair of Miss Swanson's fallen undergarments and kisses them.

Who cares about Miss Swanson? my mother said. Tell me about *my* part.

I would also hope that, as you have previously promised, you remain willing to make the acquaintance of my wife, Mister Von Stroheim said. It would, as only you can imagine, mean a great deal to her.

His wife was burned bad, my mother said to me. Now she has a face worse than mine.

Angelina appeared, curtsied, and, lifting my mother's veil, she kissed her once on each cheek, then held the veil up so that Gloria could do the same.

Mister Von Stroheim clicked his heels again, and bowed to both Gloria and Angelina.

So now that we are all here, and the sun has set, and the Sabbath is over, we can to begin, yes? Karl said, and he walked to the back of the room, switched off the lights, and turned on the projector.

When, in the darkness that surrounded us, the elderly

men and women who sat in the lounge saw a rectangle of white light tremble on the small moving picture screen, they applauded.

Upon the white rectangle, the word GREED appeared, and then, PERSONALLY DIRECTED BY ERICH VON STROHEIM, and after this, by itself: "Dedicated To My Mother."

But I've already seen this one, my mother said. We saw it at the Strand, Karl, remember?

Yes, Karl said. But what we saw was the cut-down version.

Only ten reels, Mister Von Stroheim stated. They cut my work from forty-two reels to ten. They were barbarians.

Karl explained that, since showing forty-two reels would last for at least ten hours, we would not, of course, watch the entire moving picture in one evening, but would see them at discrete intervals. Karl also said that in his opinion Mister Von Stroheim was the genius Griffith wished he had been, and that one good result of the coming of sound to moving pictures was that it had destroyed Griffith. And if we could eliminate the silent strip on the film where they store sound, he said, we could go back to shooting at the rate of sixteen frames a second instead of twenty-four, and our films would be clear and brilliant again.

Yes, Mister Von Stroheim said. Exactly.

While, upon the screen, we watched the story move forward—McTeague being tender to a little bird, then hurling a man into the river; McTeague putting Trina to sleep in his dentist's chair so that he can ravish her while she's under the influence of ether—I felt happy in the way I'd felt when I was a boy sitting in a dark theater, lost in the light and shadows that moved upon the screen.

My mother took my hand in hers. I love you, she said in the most natural of voices. No matter what. You know that, don't you, Joey?

Yes, I said.

Joey's a good boy, Gloria said.

Oh yes, my mother said. My Joey was always a good boy, even when he was a girl.

We sat next to one another on a stone bench—Mister Von Stroheim, Gloria, Angelina, my mother—while Karl paced back and forth in front of a small fountain of goldfish, and explained his plan.

What he intended to do was to buy up all the old silent pictures he could find and sell them to those places, around the globe, where sound and words did not matter—to homes for the deaf, to orphanages, to nursing homes. The Greeks— Skouras and the others—already had a lock on distribution and theater circuits, but it was Karl's belief that even if sound lasted, people would still hunger for stories without words, because without words, he claimed, you had a way of telling stories anywhere in the world without the need for transla- tion. Without words, he said—without people *hearing* what people on the screen said—the most important things were still left to the imagination.

There is a sequence in my new moving picture, Mister Von Stroheim said to my mother, wherein the mother chases Miss Swanson down a staircase while whipping her with a long leather lash. I had you in mind for the part of the mother.

Can I use a real whip?

Of course, Mister Von Stroheim said. In my films there are no illusions.

I heard the squeak of wooden wheels, turned, and saw Eva coming toward us, pushed forward into the courtyard by a nurse.

Eva weighed more than two hundred pounds now, and yet, in the round dough-like flesh of her face I could still see the beautiful woman she had once been. She was dressed in a white linen gown, a thin red-and-black paisley bandana, like that of a pirate, covering a head upon which hair no longer grew. Yellowish fluid dripped from her eyes, and her mouth was covered with scabs.

My mother reached across from her chair to Eva's, took Eva's hands in her own.

It's good to see you again, darling, she said, and she talk-ed with Eva as if Eva could talk back to her: So how was your day today? . . . Really? . . . Well, I brought my favorite son with me, like I promised, so he could say good night to you . . . You've been expecting him? . . . He does? Every week? . . . Well, isn't that sweet of him . . . Oh yes, I agree with you one hundred percent, but if you want my honest opinion, child, given what life has in store for some of us, *your* idea is best of all: eat, sleep, move your bowels comfortably at least once a day, and leave the rest to God.

My mother introduced Eva to Mister Von Stroheim, and told her that he was German.

I am not German, Mister Von Stroheim said. I am Vien-nese.

Mister Von Stroheim's like my son, my mother explained to Eva. He makes up his life as he goes along. Sometimes he's a German and sometimes he's a nobleman, and sometimes he's a student from Heidelberg and sometimes he's a military officer and at other times — well, who knows? — but the main thing is that nobody ever knows what's true about him and what's not.

Mister Von Stroheim lifted my mother's gloved hand again, but this time touched his lips to the skin of her wrist, and when he did, I thought of the wedding feast in *Greed*, where the guests feed on flesh, skulls, and fresh fruit, where they bite into one another's necks and chew on one another's fingers.

It's time for me to go, I said to my mother. I'll wheel you to the automobile.

Pay some attention to your sweetheart, my mother said.

May I escort you home? Mister Von Stroheim said to my mother.

Gloria was beside me, her hand resting lightly on my hip.

Come, I said to Eva, kissing her on the forehead. It's your bedtime. I'll see you again next week.

Oh Joey, my mother said, if you're going to kiss a wom-an, please do it the right way.

I lowered my head, kissed Eva on her mouth.

A most tender moment, Mister Von Stroheim said.

As soon as I take Eva back to her room, I'll join you again, I said. I released the brake on Eva's wheelchair, and began pushing it toward the door.

My mother stroked Angelina's hair. Now once upon a time, you see, she said, my son Joey was almost as pretty as you are, and then one day. . . .

I pushed Eva's wheelchair to the doorway, then glanced back over my shoulder. My mother lifted her right hand and, opening and closing her fist like a little girl, waved good-bye.

When the lights came on again, and Eduardo stood and bowed to the applause and shouts of his family—"*Viva Eduardo! Viva Villa! Viva Mexico!*"—Angelina asked if it was time to go and fetch her mother. I said that it was.

When, several minutes later, Gloria entered the room, Eduardo's relatives stopped their talking, and looked at her in awe, as if in the presence of a goddess. The young girls gaped, while many of the older women crossed themselves.

Gloria's face was pale, like alabaster, though the slight plum-colored flush in her cheeks told me she had been crying. She wore a long diaphanous robe of lavender chiffon— the robe she had worn when she played Esther in Karl's production of *Queen Esther and the Jews*, which had been the final movie-without-sound he had made. Her neck was bare, a diamond-studded tiara, on black velvet, atop her hair, so that, the velvet covering most of her head, it appeared that her hair had returned to its true color. Karl took her by the arm, led her to the front row, sat her down between me and Angelina. He gestured to everyone to be seated, then stood in front of the moving picture screen.

In order to celebrate the good news that I told you about before, for which Lady Eleanora and I accept your warm congratulations, I have decided that tonight I will show you something nobody on earth has ever before seen.

Karl turned out the lights and switched on the projector.

To either side of me, Gloria and Angelina held my hands. On the screen a horse-drawn sleigh appeared and it moved around a frozen lake, a mother and an infant sitting in the sleigh upon blocks of ice that were covered in burlap. The quality of the film was excellent: clear, with sharp and distinct contrasts, and without unnecessary shadows.

But . . . but it's *you*, Gloria said. It's *you*, Joey! It's *you*!

How can you tell? Angelina asked, and then: Is that Aunt Hannah?

Each time the sleigh moved around the lake and returned, the child was a year older, and each time I watched the sleigh come toward us, I heard expressions of surprise and delight come from Angelina, Eduardo, and the others, and then their awed whisperings: *Magia . . . ! Magia maravilloso . . . !*

Gloria stood, so that her shadow, taller than the moving picture, blocked out the images of me and my mother.

Why are you doing this? she asked Karl.

Be quiet, Mommy, Angelina said. And sit down. We can't *see*—

In the bright, blinding light of the projector's lamp, I saw Karl shrug, and put out his hands sideways, palms up, in a gesture of helplessness. Time-lapse perhaps, he said. I'm sorry I am displeasing you. Maybe this wasn't such a hot idea.

I followed Gloria from the room.

Gloria walked swiftly through her rose garden, across the lawn, and down to the edge of the pond that lay below her balcony. I stood next to her and when she turned to me I saw that there were tears in her eyes.

Listen, she said. Could you do me a favor and for once in your life stop being such a goddamned good boy and just hold me?

Then she was in my arms, and I was unable to stop myself from thinking of the paths that moved through the forest, on the other side of the pond, and of how, if you started on one path—the way you started at the beginning of one story, with a single image or word—and if you kept going, you would keep diverging further and further from all the other paths that might have led you into the forest. I tried to imagine all the possible paths there were, and of which one I would choose—for me, and for Gloria, and for Angelina. . . .

So listen, Gloria said. I was thinking about Karl's favorite story—the one where two men are lost in the desert and one of them has enough water to save one of them, and how Karl says the rabbis ask if he should share the water with his friend—do you remember?

Yes, I said. The rabbis say that the man should take all the water for himself, and thereby save his own life.

What I decided, see, is that's what we should do. We should save ourselves and leave Karl behind—alive or dead, what's the difference? He's had a full life is the way I look at it, and we're just getting started, you and me. We could figure it out so we get to have his studio and this place and the money too—or we could just take off, you, me, and Angelina.

There was a sudden, loud burst of applause from inside the house that caused birds to rise from the trees and take flight across the pond, heading back over our heads before turning west, toward the ocean.

You know what I worry about most of all? I said.

Tell me.

You'll think I'm silly.

Tell me.

What I worry about isn't you and the baby, or if it's mine or Karl's, or if my father and Ben are really dead or not, or about my mother or Eva, or about what Angelina's life will be like when she's old enough to leave home, but what I worry about is what, if I stop making moving pictures, I'm going to do with my life.

But we don't have to *do* anything if we don't want to, Gloria said. We can just leave things the way they are, and keep living the lives we're living, and see what happens next. I mean, it was just an idea—just a story I was making up I thought we could try on for a while, you and me. Who knows? Maybe it's enough to be friends, like I was saying this morning.

Was that this morning?

Gloria laughed. I think I know what you mean, she said.

We sat on a grassy slope beside the pond, Gloria's head on my lap.

Maybe we can take turns, she said. You tell me a story and then I'll tell you one, and then we go back and forth for as long as we want, only when it comes to a story with Karl in it, let's not forget that having a dead husband is nothing new for me, right?

What I decided, I said, is that the only thing I've ever been good at is pretending I'm other people.

But it's not so.

Shh, I said. Listen to me. What I worry about is that if I'm always being other people, even if they're in stories I make up, then who am *I*?

Oh Joey! Gloria said. Can't you see why I loved you the way I did, from that first crazy night in the cemetery when I felt like I could tell you everything?

No.

Gloria stood, reached down for me. Come, she said. Let's go home. You need some time to think—you need some time to get ready to tell me you like my plan.

I stood.

Where's home? I asked.

Yeah, she said. I think I know what you mean.

We walked around the pond once, holding hands, and then up a small grassy incline. We heard the guests, on the far side of the house, saying their farewells to one another, and we heard horses whinnying, children crying, automobile-horns honking. Angelina, in a feathery gown that looked ice-blue in the moonlight, was standing on Gloria's balcony waving to us.

We waved back, and even when we saw Karl walking down the hill toward us, we continued to hold hands, and all the while we walked toward the house I found that I was opening doors and walking through the rooms inside my head, one after the other, and setting fire to each of them, and to all the objects and stories and memories that were in them, until, when we reached Karl, and he stepped between us, turned, and put his arms around the two of us, and the three of us walked toward our home, everything inside me I had ever stored there was in flames, burning as high as the sky, straight through to heaven.

About the Author

Jay Neugeboren is the author of nineteen books, including two prize-winning novels (*The Stolen Jew, Before My Life Began*), two award-winning books of nonfiction (*Imagining Robert, Transforming Madness*), and four collections of award-winning stories. His stories and essays have appeared in *The New York Review of Books, The New York Times, The Atlantic Monthly, The American Scholar, Ploughshares, The Gettysburg Review, Virginia Quarterly Review,* and in more than fifty anthologies, including *Best American Short Stories* and *O. Henry Prize Stories.* He is the only author to have won six consecutive Syndicated Fiction Prizes, and his novel, *1940,* was long-listed for the 2009 International Impac Dublin Literary Prize. He lives in New York City.

Also by Jay Neugeboren

Novels

Big Man
Listen Ruben Fontanez
Sam's Legacy
An Orphan's Tale
The Stolen Jew
Before My Life Began
Poli: A Mexican Boy in Early Texas
1940
The Other Side of the World

Stories

Corky's Brother
Don't Worry About the Kids
News from the New American Diaspora
You Are My Heart

Nonfiction

Parentheses: An Autobiographical Journey
The Story of STORY Magazine (as editor)

Imagining Robert: My Brother, Madness, and Survival
Transforming Madness: New Lives for People Living with Mental Illness
Open Heart: A Patient's Story of Life-Saving Medicine and Life-Giving Friendship
The Hillside Diary and Other Writings (as editor)